HIGH CRIMES

THE AUGUST HIGH THRILLERS
BOOK 1

DAN AMES

A USA TODAY BESTSELLING BOOK

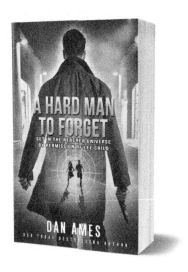

Book One in The JACK REACHER Cases

CLICK HERE TO BUY NOW

FREE BOOKS AND MORE

Would you like a FREE copy
of my story BULLET RIVER and the chance
to win a free Kindle?

Then sign up for the DAN AMES BOOK CLUB:

For special offers and new releases, sign up here

PRAISE FOR DAN AMES

"Packed to the gills with hard-hitting action and a non-stop plot." –Jacksonville News

"A fast-paced, unpredictable mystery with an engaging narrator and a rich cast of original supporting characters." –New York Times best-selling author Thomas Perry

"Dan Ames writes fast-paced, gripping tales that capture you from Page One and hold you enthralled till the last word. He brings a strong, clear voice to whichever genre he chooses. This guy is one hell of a storyteller. Watch for him." -Amazon Review

Dan Ames' writing reminds me of the great thriller writers -- lean, mean, no nonsense prose that gets straight to the point and keeps you turning those pages." –Robert Gregory Browne

These Jack Reacher stories are packed with

action and unforgettable twists and turns. Great reads! -B & N Review

"Cuts like a knife." -Savannah Morning News

"Grabs you early on and doesn't let go." - Tom Schreck

"From its opening lines, Daniel S. Ames and his private eye novel DEAD WOOD recall early James Ellroy: a fresh attitude and voice and the heady rush of boundless yearning and ambition. Ames delivers a vivid evocation of time and place in a way that few debut authors achieve, nailing the essence of his chosen corner of high-tone Michigan. He also deftly dodges the pitfalls that make so much contemporary private detective fiction a mixed bag and nostalgia-freighted misfire. Ames' detective has family; he's steady. He's not another burned-out, booze-hound hanging on teeth and toenails to the world and smugly wallowing in his own ennui. This is the first new private eye novel in a long time that just swept me along for the ride. Ames is definitely one to watch." — Craig McDonald, Edgar-nominated author

"Dan Ames pulls off a very difficult thing: he re-imagines what a hardboiled mystery can be, and does it with style, thrills and humor. This is the kind of book mystery readers are clamoring for, a fast-paced story with great heart and not a cliché to be found." -- Jon A. Jackson, author of Badger Games

"Dan Ames is a sensation among readers who love fast-paced thrillers." – Mystery Tribune

"A smart detective story stuffed with sharp prose and great action." –Indie Reader

HIGH CRIMES

An August High Thriller

by

Dan Ames

PART ONE

CHAPTER
ONE

MY NAME IS AUGUST HIGH.

Unusual, right?

It tends to breed tons of bad jokes. As in, "Are you high?"

Why yes, I am High.

If you're wondering about the story behind it, I'll tell you right now. It's not very glamorous. My mother was a drunk and a drug addict, and when she wandered into the emergency room, already starting to give birth, there was no sign of a husband or boyfriend anywhere in sight. The nurses threw her in a room and out I popped.

A nurse with a sense of humor, or maybe just a mean streak, put down High as the surname. And then for the first name she put August, since it was August first.

I suppose she could have considered a middle name.

August Really High.

August Sky High.

But I guess she didn't want to put in the effort to take the joke that far.

Which is fine by me.

Supposedly, the woman who gave birth to me died a few days later of an overdose. The doctors said I was a miracle: a huge baby, weighing in at around ten pounds with no signs of a disability.

Yeah, they didn't know me that well.

It was midnight in the middle-of-nowhere Detroit. In case you're wondering, that applies to huge sections of the city comprised entirely of abandoned homes. The long grass supports a large population of pheasants. And rodents, most likely. There's garbage everywhere. Suburbanites love to come into neighborhoods like this and toss out their hazardous waste, that way they don't have to pay to go to some fancy county site. I've seen tons of refrigerators, paint cans by the thousands, scary-looking asbestos tiles and pipes. It's like the air is dangerous, too.

A while back, some enterprising artists decided to commandeer an abandoned warehouse and make it some kind of communal studio. Not a bad idea, until a kid from France was painting outside, looking for that perfect light, when a twelve-year-old gangbanger with a .357 Magnum put a few rounds into him. Life imitates art, I guess. Anyway, only a few hardy souls still have the balls to frequent the place.

One of them, apparently, was a young woman who needed my help.

She was an artist who went by one name: Holla.

Interesting.

Anyway, she knew a friend of mine who's a bartender at The Twelve, a blues bar downtown, and said friend gave Holla my number. I talked to her briefly and she wanted me to come and meet her at the warehouse. She was scared. No surprise there. A young woman in this part of the city, especially if she was white, would be considered prey. I had no idea what Holla looked like, so I was keeping an open mind.

The abandoned warehouse emerged out of the inky night, its brick walls adorned with the work of local artists. Meaning, graffiti.

Bags of trash were scattered here or there and there was a main door into the building with a single overhead light.

As I got closer, I could smell weeds—the actual ones, you know, plants. Not ganja. The air was moist. Detroit could get super hot in the summer.

The empty, broken windows of the building seemed to follow my progress as I finally reached the door. Its steel surface was adorned with additional layers of graffiti, a palimpsest of urban expression that had accumulated over the years. I placed my hand on the door, feeling the coolness of the metal, and pushed. It creaked open with surprising ease, as if one of the artists had a can of WD-40 in his artistic arsenal.

The interior hit me with a wall of sensory input. The air carried the musty scent of damp concrete, underlaid with something sharper, almost chemical. It was a mixture of paint, solvent, and something else. Strings of lights crisscrossed the cavernous space, their cool blue glow creating an otherworldly atmosphere. The light played off the surfaces of discarded machinery and half-finished art installations, casting long shadows that seemed to move of their own accord.

"Holla?" I called out, feeling stupid doing so.

Nothing. No answer.

I called again and all I heard was a faint echo.

I navigated through the debris, my footsteps echoing in the vast space. Piles of rusted gears and splintered lumber shared space with abstract sculptures and unfinished canvases. The warehouse looked exactly like what it was: an underground creative space left abandoned once again, leaving behind this strange fusion of industrial past and artistic ambition.

A faint sound caught my attention—white noise, barely perceptible but omnipresent. I traced it to a hidden speaker system, likely left running by the last occupants. It was cheap and filthy, and I couldn't believe it was still running.

I shut it off.

Now even more eerie, I moved through the space, careful not to step anywhere that might have broken glass or razor blades.

And then in a closed-off space I saw something pale. It almost seemed to glow out of the darkness.

The feeling inside wasn't good, and it was growing stronger by the second.

As I got closer, I felt a sense of relief. It wasn't a body, it was some kind of strange art piece. A sculpture using–

Ah shit, I thought.

It was a woman.

She had been hung by her ankles and cut open from crotch to sternum like a field-dressed deer. Her arms had been pinned to metal rods that stuck out horizontal from her body. It looked like she was in the middle of a swan dive.

The smell was atrocious.

There was paint splashed across her body and her face was bloody. It definitely wasn't red paint.

Below her were entrails and they appeared to have been pushed around to make some kind of morbid design. I touched the edge of a blood pool with my finger. The blood was fresh. She hadn't been dead long.

One of the lights above had partially detached, swinging gently in a non-existent breeze. It cast shifting patterns of light and shadow across the dead girl, alternately revealing and concealing the grim presence of death.

The girl's dark brown hair had been splattered with some kind of fluorescent paint that caught the reflection of the bluish-tined light and made the scene even more bizarre.

As I knelt beside her, careful not to disturb any potential evidence, I studied her eyes. They too were dark brown, still open, and looked almost purplish in the light. A smear of pink paint trailed from her mouth to her ear, as if someone had tried to make her die with a big grin on her face.

Her hands, adorned with chipped gel nails in a shade of crimson that now seemed darkly prophetic, were frozen in a gesture that looked part defensive, part accusatory.

The subtle indentations on her neck suggested a thin wire or cord. Hopefully, she had been dead before they strung her up.

This wasn't just a murder; it was a carefully orchestrated scene. The unsettling silence continued, broken only by the soft hum of the lights.

Before calling the police, I used the flashlight on my phone to study her more closely. It looked like there was a light series of tattoos on her leg. A design of some sort. It was difficult to guess her age, early twenties probably, but the margin of error was large.

I was about to put my phone away when something caught my eye in the horrible tableau beneath the victim. Amongst the blood and tissue and organs, a small corner of yellow could be seen.

Carefully, I plucked it out from its resting space and saw it was a slip of paper. I carried it over to the stereo system where the light was best. There was writing on the paper, but it was hard to read, if not impossible. There was a piece of fabric on the floor just a few feet away. I picked it up and placed the paper inside it, then carefully rolled the fabric up and put it in my pocket.

As I pushed open the warehouse door to call the cops, the warm night air hit me like a welcome relief.

I called the cops and told them what I'd found. In this part of the city, it might take an hour or two, or they might not come at all.

If that was Holla who'd been killed, she had certainly been right.

She'd had good reason to be scared.

CHAPTER TWO

THE FLICKERING STREETLIGHT cast uneven pools of sickly yellow light on the cracked pavement, creating a patchwork of illumination and shadow. The distant hum of city traffic, even at this hour of the night, provided a low, constant backdrop—a reminder of the still-living world beyond this forsaken corner. The air was thick with the acrid smell of decay and abandonment, tinged with the metallic scent of approaching rain.

As I waited, the first uniformed officers arrived, their patrol cars slicing through the darkness with flashing red and blue lights that briefly illuminated the grim surroundings. The sudden burst of color seemed almost obscene against the monochromatic gloom of the warehouse district. The artists would have loved the juxtaposition. Maybe even the composition, too.

I watched as two cops emerged from the police cruiser. They came up to me.

"You call in a body?" one of them asked. They were both young and barrel-chested and strong. Lots of tattoos on their forearms. Detroit cops were no joke.

But they were smaller than me. I could tell they weren't used to that.

"Yeah, she's in there. I warn you, though, it's not a pretty sight."

"Go ahead," the one on the left said. "I'll take his statement."

I supplied the usual information and identification and he jotted it all down in a little notebook. He asked if I knew who the girl was. I said her name was Holla, as far as I knew.

He looked up at me to see if I was serious, then wrote it down. He was going to ask me something else but suddenly there was a shout from inside.

"Wait here," the cop said. Not great operating procedure. If I was the killer I could just take off, even if I'd called it in.

Both cops came out, one of them wiping his mouth.

If he contaminated the crime scene, the homicide detective who was sure to arrive wouldn't appreciate it.

"What the hell?" one of them asked me.

I just shrugged my shoulders.

Twenty minutes passed. I wish I smoked so it would help pass the time. Another twenty passed and then a Buick sedan pulled up. A woman got out. Not too tall, not too short. Her black skin blended into the night. She had on blue jeans, a white t-shirt and a light leather jacket. It was more like a sport coat than anything.

The two cops huddled with her and then left to get crime scene tape, I assumed.

She ignored me and walked into the building. Another twenty minutes passed. The coroner's van pulled up. They walked by me without comment.

A full hour later the detective came back. This time, she addressed me.

"I'm Detective Monroe," she said. The streetlight caught the glint of her badge and I took note of the number.

She had a strong chin and face-to-face, I realized she was striking in an elegant and unusual kind of way. Her body was solid and athletic. Her hair was short with a slight wave to it.

A dog barked somewhere in the distance, the sound echoing off the abandoned buildings. A siren wailed far away, rising and falling like a mournful cry.

"Your name is August High?" she asked, one eyebrow slightly raised.

"It sure is."

I waited for the inevitable joke. Some pun on smoking pot.

No joke came.

"That name sounds familiar."

There was no need for me to respond.

"I need to know why you're here," she said.

"A friend of mine gave my number to a girl who said she needed help. She called me just after midnight, said she was in trouble and needed someone to meet her here. I came down, and when I got inside, I found her like that."

Monroe's eyes narrowed slightly. "And you didn't recognize her?" she asked, her tone neutral but probing.

"Never saw her before in my life," I replied.

Monroe's gaze shifted back to the warehouse, her expression thoughtful.

"What's the name of your friend?"

"Jazz. Actually, Jasmine Park, a bartender at The Twelve." I'd already told the uniforms this, but she was just checking to see if I'd change my story.

"Did the girl say who she was afraid of?"

"Nope."

"And what was the girl's name?"

Monroe studied me for a moment, her eyes seeming to come to a decision.

"All right, Mr. High," she said finally. "I appreciate your cooperation. I'll need your contact information."

"I already gave it to them," I said, pointing toward the uniforms.

"Give it to me," she said. "Just in case."

As I provided my contact details, Monroe pulled out a small notebook, jotting down the information with quick, efficient strokes. Her pen moved across the page with a smooth precision. I got the feeling she did everything smoothly.

"I'll be in touch if we need anything further. For now, you're free to go, but I advise against leaving the area until our investigation is complete."

Sure," I said. "I'll be around if you need me."

As Monroe turned to leave, I caught a glimpse of something in her eyes – a flicker of fatigue, or annoyance, or humor. She returned to the warehouse, her figure receding into the shadows, swallowed up by the looming darkness of the building.

Weaving my way through the crime scene technicians, I walked back to my car. It was a Ford Maverick from the seventies. It was sort of plain, but it was a monster on the road thanks to some customizing. I never really worried about it getting stolen or broken into in a neighborhood like this. It didn't exactly reek of wealth.

I turned the key in the ignition, the engine rumbling to life. As I pulled away from the curb, I cast one last glance at the warehouse in my rearview mirror. The flashing lights of the police cars had ceased.

The city's darkness seemed to close in as I drove, even though sunrise was on its way.

A new day a dead girl hung by her feet hadn't lived to see.

CHAPTER
THREE

ALL WAS quiet when I parked the Mav in my assigned spot. My loft was located on the top floor of a converted warehouse near downtown Detroit. I avoided the elevator and climbed the metal steps and glanced over at the building next door, a furniture store full of stuff that looked incredibly uncomfortable.

My door was formidable, not going to lie. I salvaged one of the original doors from the warehouse, had it cut to size and steel reinforced. The locks were industrial, too. It would take a master thief with an unlimited budget for power tools to get in through the front door.

Once inside, I went to my room I call the

armory and hung up my pistol. After that, I took a long, hot shower. Can you blame me?

Afterward, I poured myself three fingers of whiskey and walked into my main space. It was open and airy, with high ceilings and exposed brick walls that hinted at the building's origins. A sleek, modern kitchen was tucked into one corner, its surfaces clean and uncluttered. I'd never been much of a cook and couldn't remember the last time I'd used any of the appliances. The coffeemaker, on the other hand, was in constant use.

I'd kept the place simple: a leather sofa, a low glass coffee table, and a few functional pieces of furniture. The floor was polished concrete, its surface reflecting the dim light from the industrial-style fixtures hanging overhead. The only signs of life were my neatly arranged home gym equipment and the martial arts gear I'd set up against one wall.

The air was cool and still, a stark contrast to the humid night outside. I took the blood-stained note out of my pocket and put it on the coffee table, the crumpled fabric falling to the floor. The note was smeared with blood, its message barely legible. I spread it out and examined it closely, but the writing was a jumbled mess of ink and blood. The more I studied it, the less sense it made. The letters were blurred, the meaning obscured by the gruesome circumstances of its origin. I wondered how best to decipher whatever was written on it.

It was important, though.

Because I had a gut feeling the dead girl had eaten the note just before she knew she was going to be killed.

I rubbed my eyes, feeling the faint waves of fatigue. I never slept much, though. As a kid, too many weird dreams and somehow, the habit just continued on.

I settled into my favorite leather chair, the whiskey giving way to an illusory sense of relaxation. The chair faced large windows and parts of the city were visible. I took another sip of whiskey, letting the warmth spread through my body.

My mind drifted back to the crime scene.

I dozed off in the chair for a few hours, which is usually the most sleep I can get.

Even then, I had a weird dream involving a bizarre sculpture of dead girls. No surprise there.

In the kitchen I brewed a pot of the good stuff, enjoyed the smell of it as it filled the space.

I drank the coffee black, savoring the bitter taste.

Once the coffee was finished, I moved to my home gym. The heavy bag was my first stop. I wrapped my hands and began to work out, the rhythmic thud of my punches echoing through the loft. The workout was intense, a way to channel my frustration and unease into something productive. My movements were precise and controlled, a reflection of years of training. Notice I didn't say discipline. I'd never been a disciplined fighter. Good? Yes. Disciplined? No.

After the heavy bag, I moved on to the weights, which were really a form of meditation.

As I finished my last set, I caught a glimpse of myself in the mirror. The man staring back at me was a beast. Remember when I said I'd been a ten-pound baby? Well, that kid grew up to be six and a half feet tall and nearly three hundred pounds. Most of it muscle.

The face? Well, the face wasn't pretty.

Too many fights involving fists, brass knuckles and knives. I had some scars here and there, and if my nose had an original shape, I had no idea what it might have been. The eyes were as blue as the Caribbean Sea, which I'd never seen, but someone had told me that. Maybe one day I could make the comparison in person.

When I was finished with the workout, I showered again, letting the hot water wash away the sweat and some of the tension in my muscles. I dressed in casual clothes—jeans, a gray T-shirt. In the armory, I put on the usual: a shoulder holster with my .45 auto, and an ankle holster with a five-shot compact .357 Magnum. Lastly, a knife tucked into my front pocket. After that I added a light leather jacket, not unlike Detective Monroe's, mostly to conceal the shoulder holster. I smiled at her memory and couldn't tell you why.

As I headed out, I thought about who I was going to see and the last time I'd seen him. It had to have been at least two months or so. His name was Paul Fawcett and he had been a cop once, one of the best. A bullet had left him paralyzed a decade ago. Now, he worked as a freelance investigator, mostly on the cyber side of it. I used him a lot because I didn't own a computer, although people keep telling me my phone is practically a computer all by itself.

The day was overcast, the sky a dull gray that often lingers in Detroit. I climbed into the Maverick and headed across town to Paul's place.

He lived on the west side, in a quiet part of town, a stark contrast to the industrial grit of the warehouse district where I lived. His house was a classic brick bungalow, probably built in the 1920s, and was always immaculate, with neat landscaping. The house had been adapted for his needs, with a ramp and wide doorways to accommodate his wheelchair.

I parked in front of his house and made my way to the front door where Paul's voice came through the intercom before I could knock. "August, come on in."

The door opened automatically, and I stepped into the house. The interior was carefully arranged, with plenty of room for Paul to navigate. The living room was spacious and comfortable, with a large sectional sofa and a television, and special equipment to let him operate everything.

"Back here!" he called.

Paul was waiting for me in his wheelchair, positioned at his desk. He pretty much lived in the room. There was a bunch of police memorabilia on the wall. Photos, awards, and newspaper articles.

He had loved being a cop.

"August. It's been a while." He smiled. He was overweight now, even though he'd been built like a linebacker before the shooting. He had a head of messy salt-and-pepper hair and a white beard.

"Yeah," I said. "Too long."

I settled into a chair across from his desk, and Paul maneuvered his wheelchair closer. His desk was cluttered with computer equipment—monitors, keyboards, and various gadgets. It was clear that this was his domain, a place where he turned his technical skills into a form of expertise that I had come to rely on over the years.

We made idle chat for a little bit and then

when there was a lull he said, "Whatcha got for me?"

I pulled the bloodstained note from my pocket and placed it on the desk in front of him. "I found this at a crime scene last night. It's a mess, but there might be something in there. I know there's writing. But that's about it. I figured maybe with your scanners and computer stuff, you could see what I can't."

"That's a lot of blood," he said.

"Yeah, I think the victim ate it before she was killed."

He glanced over at me. "Jesus," he said.

Paul examined the note. "It's a mess, all right. I can clean it up a bit on the computer, but there's no guarantee we'll get anything coherent."

"Do what you can," I said.

Paul leaned back. "This have anything to do with that girl I heard was strung up and gutted like a caribou?"

"No comment," I replied.

He laughed. "Yeah, that's not something I would comment on, either."

We sat in silence for a few moments.

"How long do you need?" I asked. "You pretty busy?"

"Not bad," he replied. "Give me a day or two."

"Perfect," I said.

I stood up and Paul left me with a bit of advice.

"Be careful out there," he said. "You never know."

We both knew exactly what he meant.

CHAPTER
FOUR

OUTSIDE OF PAUL'S house the sight of the blue sky was a welcome sight. Sometimes the dull gray dome over Detroit felt like a trap. But when it lifted, it was easier to breathe.

As I approached the Mav, a young woman approached. She had clearly been waiting outside, standing near the sidewalk. She clutched a notepad and a pen, her gaze fixed on me with an intensity that suggested she had been waiting for some time.

Her expression was a mix of curiosity and determination. Her blonde hair was pulled back into a tight ponytail, and her professional attire—blouse and slacks—was neatly pressed. She looked to be in her early twenties, fresh-faced and earnest.

"Excuse me," she said, her voice clear and assertive. "Are you August High?"

I gave her a nod, maintaining a steady pace toward the driver's side of my car. "That's right."

"I'm Gretchen Mercer," she said, holding out her hand. "I'm a journalist. I was hoping to ask you a few questions."

"Nothing about me is worthy of the news," I said. "Unless it's bad news."

Gretchen's gaze remained unwavering, her pen poised over her notepad. "I understand, but I've been following a murder case. It occurred last night and your name was mentioned."

"Really?" I asked. "By whom"

"That's not important."

"To you it isn't."

"Were you there?"

"I was with my Buddhist group, meditating."

She looked up at me, took in my size, my face.

"Did you know the girl?" she asked.

"What girl?"

"Hala Yousef. H-A-L-A."

Holla, I thought. Probably a different spelling for her artistic identity.

"Nope."

Her eyes narrowed slightly, but she didn't back down. "I heard the cops were hassling Pulse. Any idea why?"

"Who?"

"Pulse," Gretchen said, her eyes rolling. "My God, are you a caveman? Everyone in Detroit has heard of him."

I didn't respond immediately, just started the engine.

"Do you have any raw meat on you?" I asked.

She looked at me, clearly annoyed. I made a grunting sound and shifted the Maverick into gear, burning no small amount of rubber as I pulled away. I could see her watching me through the rearview mirror, her expression a mix of frustration and determination.

Once I was a few blocks away, I pulled over and dialed Paul's number. The line rang a couple of times before he answered.

"You again?" he asked. "Miss me already?"

"Yeah, sorry," I said, "I need an address for

some artist called Pulse the cops were hassling. Can you find it for me and text me as soon as you can?"

"Sure. This case is a weird one, isn't it?" he asked.

"Yeah," I replied.

We disconnected and I pointed the Mav in the general direction of the city. I figured no pretentious artist would live in West Bloomfield.

Sure enough, my phone buzzed and I saw an address on West River Road. I knew the street.

Glancing behind me occasionally to see if the intrepid Gretchen Mercer was following me, I made it to West River Street in no time. The building was a gigantic Victorian (guessing here) that was probably built at the turn of the century. It was enormous, with three turrets, a slate roof, a huge porch that wrapped around the building, and exquisite landscaping with a bunch of weird sculptures everywhere.

Some of them looked familiar to something I'd just seen.

I parked the car a short distance away and approached the entrance. The front door was beautiful, all hand-carved oak, I assumed. There was a buzzer system to the right. I pressed the button, and after a moment, a voice crackled through the intercom.

"Yeah?"

"Delivery for Pulse," I said. Hey, I was going to deliver some questions so there was no untruthfulness involved.

After a brief silence, the intercom clicked off. The door unlocked with a faint click, and I pushed it open, stepping into the lobby. The space was sleek and minimalistic, with modern art pieces displayed on the walls. The atmosphere was a sharp contrast to the exterior architecture of the place.

The lobby led into a large open studio area, filled with canvases, paint supplies, and various sculptures. Pulse seemed to enjoy a chaotic mix of creativity and mess, with paint splatters decorating the floor and walls. The whole thing had an air of arrogance, the kind that comes with a self-important artist.

I took a moment to survey the scene. The studio was busy, with a few assistants moving around, but the artist himself was easy to spot. Pulse was a tall man in his mid-forties, with an air of confidence about him. He was slender, effeminate and dressed in purple silk. Not a kimono. Not a bathrobe. I had no idea what it was.

Beside him stood a large man—his bodyguard, I assumed. The bodyguard filled the space around him. He wore a dark suit that was ill-fitting, which surprised me. I figured Pulse would demand fashion perfection from his employees.

An assistant appeared before me, a young man, or woman, I couldn't tell, with a nose ring. "Where's the delivery?" he/she asked.

"Oh, I left it by the door."

Ignoring the assistant, I walked right up to the great man himself. Pulse. His real name was probably Chuck Miller or something like that.

He looked at me, his flat gray eyes narrowing with a mixture of curiosity and wariness. "Can I help you?" he asked, his voice carrying a hint of impatience. He was standing before a canvas that looked like someone with irritable bowel syndrome had used as a diaper.

"I'm looking for Holla."

"Oh my sweet dear, you are just a smidgen too late." He smiled at me.

"Oh, she said you were a good friend of hers."

Pulse looked over at his bodyguard, who moved in closer.

I ignored the bodyguard's attempt at intimidation. "I noticed one of your sculptures out front. It looked like a person hanging upside down with their arms spread like wings. Is that yours?"

"Of course it is, you dolt," he snapped. "Why would I put someone else's pieces in my yard?"

The bodyguard's patience wore thin. He stepped forward, his large hands reaching for me. I saw his move coming and reacted calmly. I stepped back, maintaining a safe distance.

"Good to know," I said to the artist. "Thank you for your time, Puss."

The bodyguard reacted instantly. He lunged forward, aiming to grab me. I stepped into it, feeling almost sorry for the guy. He'd clearly been hired for his bulk and not his fighting skill. I took a short step toward him, rocked off my back foot and threw a short, straight right hand with every ounce of my two hundred and ninety-nine point nine pounds.

The result wasn't pretty.

The sound of a jaw breaking filled the space, along with the thud of the bodyguard hitting the floor.

Pulse looked down at his employee.

"Hang him upside down," I said to him. "It'll be a cool piece. So, what can you tell me about Holla?"

"I heard a few things," he said. This guy was a cool customer. "It was late, and I was working and there was cold Chablis on tap."

"Go on," I prompted.

"Murder and drugs, is what I heard" he said. "Nothing specific. Just…murder. And drugs."

There was nothing to say. I sort of believed him. I turned to leave and the assistant came to the bodyguard's side, a look of horror on her face. Our eyes met.

"You might want to ice that," I said.

PART TWO

CHAPTER
FIVE

THE TWELVE WAS in a dingy part of Detroit. Make your own joke about the whole city being dingy. Its name came from the musical pattern of the blues called the twelve bar blues.

The place was a familiar watering hole for Detroiters, but not exactly popular. Its exterior was unassuming, with a weathered sign glowing in neon blue, flickering occasionally as if to remind passersby of its age and character. The brick facade, worn smooth by decades of Michigan weather, bore witness to countless nights of music and revelry. A small chalkboard propped against the wall announced the evening's entertainment: "Live Blues - 9 PM."

I paused for a moment before entering, taking in the muffled sounds of a harmonica drifting through the thick wooden door. A couple of patrons huddled near the entrance, sharing a cigarette and hushed conversation, their words lost in the cool evening air.

Inside, the bar's walls were lined with deep mahogany panels, their rich hue deepened by years of exposure to smoke and spirits. Framed blues memorabilia adorned every available space, telling the stories of legendary musicians who had graced stages across the country. Faded concert posters, autographed guitars, and black-and-white photographs created a visual timeline of blues history.

The air was thick with the rich aroma of bourbon and cigarettes, punctuated by the steady hum of blues music from the sound system that was shut off when live acts were in house, which was quite often. Currently, "Sweet Home Chicago," filled the room with its melancholic tones.

The lighting was low and warm, provided by a combination of vintage-style Edison bulbs hanging from the ceiling and small table lamps scattered throughout the room.

The soft glow created an intimate atmosphere, with shadows dancing on the walls as patrons moved about.

To my right, a long bar stretched the length of the room. Its surface, polished to a high shine, reflected the warm lights above, creating a golden glow that seemed to invite weary souls to rest their elbows and forget about their cheating wives, no-good husbands and horrible bosses. Behind the bar were the antidotes: rows of whiskeys, bourbons, and other spirits that gave peace to the tormented soul.

Jazz was behind the bar, her presence a central part of the bar's charm. Her real name was Jasmine Park, as I had told Detective Monroe. In her late thirties, Jazz was a stunner. Her dad was a white auto executive, her mother a Japanese engineer. The result was a happy marriage and a beautiful daughter. Jazz had on a black tank top and jeans that emphasized her petite but curvy body. Her short hair, a mix of dark brown and premature subtle gray streaks, framed her almond face and ruby lips.

Her hands moved with practiced efficiency as she mixed drinks, her fingers adorned with several silver rings that clinked softly against the glasses.

As I approached the bar, I noticed the usual crowd of regulars scattered about. In a corner booth, an older gentleman with salt-and-pepper hair nursed a glass of scotch, his eyes closed as he swayed slightly to the music. At a small table near the corner, a young couple leaned in close, their conversation punctuated by soft laughter and the occasional clink of their beer bottles.

"August," Jazz greeted me with a genuine smile, her voice carrying easily over the ambient noise. "Figured I'd see you sooner than later." Her eyes were a deep brown that invited me to a place I hoped one day I would go. But not now.

"Yeah," I replied, as I slid onto a barstool and placed my hands on the bar, feeling the coolness of the polished wood against my palms.

Jazz reached for a bottle of whiskey without asking. The amber liquid caught the light as she poured, creating a small cascade of gold in the glass. She set it down with practiced ease, the heavy-bottomed tumbler making a satisfying thud against the bar top.

"Thanks," I said. "Tell me about the girl."

"Did she call you?" Jazz had an open expression. She hadn't heard, obviously.

I took a sip of the whiskey. The flavor was rich and complex, with wood and fire that made love on the tongue.

"Yeah," I said. "But I was too late."

"What do you mean?" she asked.

There was no good way to say it. "Did you hear about the murder at the artists' place? The abandoned warehouse?"

"Oh no," Jazz said. She brought her hands to her face. "That's terrible! She seemed so nice!"

"How did you know her?" I asked.

Jazz went and poured a drink for another customer and came back.

"I didn't," she said. "She came in and looked totally lost, so I gave her a drink on the house and asked what brought her in. She said she was scared but wouldn't elaborate. I told her to go to the cops but she said she couldn't. So I gave her your number."

It was exactly as I had expected. Jazz and I went way back. I trusted her, which is no small feat.

"Anything else? Anything at all?"

Jazz shook her head, her brow furrowing in concentration. Her short hair swayed slightly with the motion, catching the warm light from above. "Not much," she admitted, her fingers drumming lightly on the bar top. "She was pretty vague. Just said she was scared and needed someone reliable. Mentioned something about her art and keeping it safe, but didn't give any more details. She said something about not even feeling safe in Ferndale, but it was loud and I didn't really hear her."

"Ferndale," I repeated, mentally noting it down. The suburb, known for its artsy vibe and eclectic community, seemed a fitting place for an artist's studio.

"Can I use the office for a bit?" I asked, draining the last of my whiskey. The glass made a hollow sound as I set it back down on the bar.

Jazz nodded, her expression softening slightly. "Sure thing. You know where it is."

I thanked her and slid off the barstool, and navigated around tables and patrons, the floorboards creaking softly under my feet.

The office was tucked away at the back of the bar, a small sanctuary away from the bustle of the main room. I opened the door, the old hinges protesting slightly, and stepped inside. This space was our shared refuge, a practical workspace amidst the bar's clutter. The office was filled with stacks of paperwork and bar-related items, but it served its purpose well enough.

The room was small, barely large enough for a desk, a filing cabinet, and a couple of chairs. The walls were a faded beige, adorned with a mismatched collection of framed photos, old concert posters, and a large cork board covered in various notes and reminders. A single window, its blinds perpetually closed, filtered in a thin stream of streetlight, creating long shadows across the cluttered space.

I dug out a new folder from the bottom drawer of the desk and wrote on the tab, *Holla*.

The next thirty minutes was spent writing down everything I had learned on sheets of paper from a yellow legal pad. When I was done, I went to the middle drawer of the file cabinet on the left and opened it. All of my case notes were alphabetized. For some reason, it always felt safer to me than keeping in my loft. Maybe one day I would get my own office. For now, it gave me a reason to come to The Twelve, have a few drinks and talk to Jazz.

That task completed, I left the office. The transition from the quiet, enclosed space back to the lively bar was jarring. The music seemed louder now, the conversations more animated. Jazz was busy behind the bar, her focus on the rapidly burgeoning crowd.

Outside the night air was warm and slightly humid, not as bad as earlier in the day. The street was quieter now, with only the occasional car passing by. The neon sign of The Twelve bar cast a soft blue glow over the sidewalk.

I made my way to the Maverick, parked a short distance down the street, but not too far from the streetlights, which provided about the only security in the area.

Firing up the big engine, I drove away from the bar, with a single destination in mind.

Ferndale.

CHAPTER SIX

THE TRANSITION from Detroit's urban sprawl to Ferndale's more subdued atmosphere was palpable, like crossing an invisible boundary into a different and funkified world. For years, Ferndale had been a neglected area just north of the city. Over the years, though, it became a hip place for young people to buy starter homes. New businesses moved in to serve the new folks and thus the community's moniker became Fashionable Ferndale.

The shops that dotted the main drag varied from used bookstores to Thai restaurants, thrift stores and vinyl record shops.

I passed a small park complete with playground equipment and park benches. A solitary figure walked a dog along the perimeter, their pace leisurely and unhurried.

Among a section of town about a block off Main Street sat Eunice, an art gallery for mostly local artists, but occasionally some recognized names or vintage pieces. The shop was named after Eunice Miller. I'd met her a long time ago when she'd needed my help and we'd stayed in touch.

The shop was a small, unassuming space with a modern facade that stood out among the more traditional buildings surrounding it. It was nestled between a cozy-looking coffee shop and a boutique clothing store.

The sign above the entrance read EUNICE in sleek, minimalist lettering. The font choice and styling suggested a contemporary focus and the main display behind glass showcased a colorful selection of paintings and sculptures of various styles and genres. I was no art expert, though, as the mostly empty walls in my loft could confirm.

There were plenty of open parking space and I guided the Mav into the first spot. Inside, I saw Eunice with either a customer or an artist, so when I got out of the car, I straightened my jacket and ran a hand through my hair, trying to make myself look more presentable. Someone told me if they ever needed to scare small children, they would just invite me over.

The subtle chime of the door announced my arrival into the hushed ambiance of the art space.

The gallery was minimalist in design, with clean lines and walls painted crisp white, providing a neutral backdrop that allowed the artwork to take center stage. Track lighting on the ceiling was angled to highlight each piece, and the air smelled like lavender.

The walls were adorned with various pieces, each one more striking than the last. Abstract paintings with bold splashes of color hung next to hyper-realistic landscapes. Sculptures of various materials – metal, wood, and what looked like repurposed industrial parts – were strategically placed throughout the space, inviting viewers to circle around and examine them from all angles.

One piece, in particular, caught my eye – a large canvas dominated by swirls of deep blue and violent red, with jagged black lines cutting through the composition. There was something unsettling about it, a sense of chaos barely contained within the frame. It was completely different than anything else in the gallery and I idly wondered if this might be one of Holla's works.

Eunice was dressed in all black like usual. A tall, striking woman with pale skin and jet-black hair. Her hair was pulled back in a neat bun, and she wore minimal jewelry – simple silver studs in her ears and a delicate white gold Rolex on her wrist.

When the person she'd been talking to moved on to study some of the artwork, she nodded me over. "August," she said. "Are you finally going to buy something or just scare off my customers."

Eunice loved to tease me about my appearance and I didn't mind one bit.

"Last time I checked, I haven't won the lottery," I said, teasing her back about the prices.

She laughed and said, "So what brings you in?"

"Do you know of an artist named Holla?"

"Sure. She's pretty well known in Detroit. That's one of hers." Sure enough, Eunice pointed out the violent piece in the window. "Why?"

"Did you know her well?"

"Why are you using the past tense?"

My face gave her the answer.

"Oh no," Eunice said.

"Yeah, sorry to break the news."

"How?"

I took a quick glance around to make sure no one was listening. "She was murdered."

Eunice closed her eyes. "Sometimes this city…"

The silence hung between us for a few moments.

"But you didn't come here just to break the news, right?" Eunice asked, after returning her gaze to me.

"No, I was wondering if you knew where her studio was located."

"Are you working the case?"

"Not really, meaning, no one is paying me."

"Oh," she said. "Hold on."

Eunice went into the back room that served as her office and I heard her shuffling around, opening and closing drawers. The comment I'd made about getting paid reminded me I needed to check my bank accounts. I'd just finished a case and the deposit should have been made by now. If not, I would need to hustle up some business.

"Here you go," Eunice said, handing me a slip of paper. It was a purchase order, with the name Hala Yousef and a Ferndale address. "It's over on the east side of town. Not a great area, but cheap."

I pocketed the paper and said, "Thanks. I'll keep you posted."

"Please do, and be careful, August."

"Always am," I replied.

The studio wasn't far, as the receptionist had said, but it was in a part of Ferndale I wasn't familiar with. Eunice was right, the area wasn't great with lots of small houses sitting among unkempt lawns, old beat-up cars parked on the street and a few abandoned buildings. It was definitely a mixed-use area with residential and industrial all thrown into an urban blender.

The building was a step up from the warehouse where Holla had been killed, but just barely. The exterior was graffiti-free but marked by faded paint and years of exposure to the elements with clearly no maintenance performed. A large, heavy door dominated the front, its metal surface showing signs of rust around the edges.

I parked in front of the building, stepped out of the car and a faint breeze washed over me, carrying the scent of damp earth and something metallic and oily.

At the front door, I saw a row of mailboxes with unit numbers. Most of them looked like they hadn't been used in years. But one of them clearly had. It was the one that matched the address on the purchase order.

Always an optimist, I tried the front door but it was locked. There was a button for an intercom but when I pressed it and spoke, nothing happened. Walking around the building, I spotted a second entrance, probably originally designed for deliveries. The large garage-style door was locked, but a smaller door to the left of it gave me an opportunity. It was locked, but the frame was warped and I could see the deadbolt barely holding. All I needed to do was lean into the door until it bowed and popped free.

Holla's studio number was 3 and as I found the main hallway, the door nearest me was marked 5.

Two doors down and I faced another locked door. A part of me was surprised there wasn't police tape on the door. Had they been here? Did they even know about the place? I hadn't heard a peep from Detective Monroe.

The small, flat leather case was inside my wallet. I took out two silver implements vaguely resembling tweezers and worked the lock. Despite the meathooks my hands resembled, I could be fairly dexterous on occasion. The door opened silently and I stepped inside, closing and locking it behind me.

The space consisted mostly of one main room, which was cluttered with various art supplies and unfinished canvases. Easels stood like sentinels throughout the space, some bearing works I couldn't tell if they were finished, or just begun.

It was a large space, with high ceilings sporting peeling paint and impressive windows, their panes dirty and/or cracked, but somehow managed to allow plenty of natural light. During a sunny day I imagined the studio would be ideal for an artist.

A workbench was covered in an array of brushes, their bristles stiff with dried paint. Jars of pigments in every conceivable color were arranged in a haphazard rainbow. Sketchbooks lay open, their pages filled with rough drawings and hastily scribbled notes. A small picture frame leaned against the wall. I picked it up and saw the real Hala Yousef, not the one hung from the ceiling of a warehouse, with an older woman. I flipped the frame over, popped off the back, lifted the photo and put it in my pocket.

The canvases I passed showed mostly geometric-type images and none of the violence of the piece I'd seen in Eunice's gallery.

Maybe I'm in the wrong place, I thought. I made a full circuit of the space, found a small, filthy bathroom and a closet that held a cot with a pillow and a few blankets.

Back in the main room, I thought something was off. The space felt right, but the paintings were wrong.

Then, partially hidden behind a large easel, I found a door. It was slightly ajar, and a sliver of light peeked through the gap. The door itself had been painted the same color as the walls, and only through sheer luck I had been able to spot it.

The room was a gallery of violent images, much more severe than the painting in Eunice's gallery. These were done with exquisite skill and detail. They were almost like photographs.

Each image depicted someone murdered and mutilated.

All of them were men.

Strung up by their feet and gutted like an animal.

CHAPTER
SEVEN

JUST DOWN THE street from Holla's studio was a gas station and convenience store. The Mav was getting low and I thought I might ask a few questions. As I filled up the tank, the steady click of the nozzle punctuated the silence. It occurred to me this particular corner probably didn't see a lot of business, being off the beaten path a bit.

As the pump finished, I replaced the nozzle, grabbed my receipt and walked into the store. The interior was cramped, which isn't saying much because with my bulk, all of these stores seem tiny. But this was ridiculous. The shelves were half-full with snacks, drinks and household essentials. Everything about the place was dirty. The floor looked like it hadn't been mopped since Ronald Reagan took office. The smell of stale coffee, body odor and either cigarettes, joints, or both filled the air. Even the lighting was bad; fluorescent bulbs flickered intermittently, which didn't help the overall vibe of the store.

Behind the counter, a clerk was stationed —dark skin, with dark hair and a beard, he was probably in his thirties and carried a look of complete disinterest. It took him nearly thirty seconds to acknowledge me standing at the counter.

He just looked at me. On the pocket of his shirt was a name I could just make out. Malik.

From my pocket, I presented the photo I'd lifted from Holla's place.

"Have you seen the younger woman in this photo around?"

He looked back at his tablet and I wasn't sure if he was going to answer. Without looking back up at me he said, "Nope."

"Are you sure?" I pressed. "She lives around here." No need to tell him she was dead, as the man appeared to care about nothing.

This time he didn't answer me at all.

"You always this busy?" I asked. There were cameras in both corners of the cashier's space, and behind the clerk I could see the reflection of monitors. They must have been beneath the counter to my right. Without a doubt there were more than two monitors, judging by their reflection. My guess was there were six. Which meant there were four other cameras somewhere.

If this place made any money, I thought, *it wasn't from selling ten-year-old bags of potato chips.*

Back outside I regretted buying my gas from the place. Oh well, I figured I would never be back.

My stomach rumbled and I drove over to Woodward Avenue, then headed south back into the city to a diner called Hank's Place. It had been there forever and it was a regular place for cops and lawyers and anyone related to crime, as the courthouse was only a few blocks away.

Inside, I was met with a wall of good smells: fried hamburger, onions, and coffee. The floor was checkerboard, the booths were red vinyl. I bypassed the booths and took a seat at the counter in the corner, mainly because I took up too much room if I sat in the middle.

The counter was polished stainless steel, with three busy waitresses and an open window into the kitchen. Orders written on a pad were tacked up so the cook could see them. He'd put a heaping tray of food on the counter and snatch the corresponding order. Carla, a server who'd worked at Hank's so long the place should have been called Carla's, came over. She was thin and wiry and if anyone asked me who should run the country, I'd tell them where to find Carla.

"Hey Big Man," she said, pouring me a fresh cup of coffee. "The truck just delivered so we should have enough for you."

Old joke, as a time or two I had put on some impressive displays of food consumption.

"Two double bacon cheeseburgers… for now."

She laughed, jotted down the order and headed to the window where she clipped it to the end of the row.

There was a newspaper folded up on the stool next to me. Reading, I learned the Lions were improving, the Pistons were falling apart and the murder rate in the city was rising.

Sounds about right, I thought.

I had made my way into the business section when Carla returned with my order. She set the plate down and the cheeseburgers were enormous, with juice dripping onto the plate next to a miniature tower of golden French fries. Lettuce, tomato and a raw onion completed the deal.

"Lunch is served," she said, refilling my coffee and adding a glass of water with a slice of lemon to the space next to my plate.

"Looks delicious, as always," I said. It tasted even better than it looked. I added some black pepper to the fries and before I knew it, the first burger was gone, all of the fries, and half of the second burger.

"You've got a lot of room to fill up," a voice next to me said. Cade Vance had slid onto the stool two spaces away from me and was now looking at me, a grin on his face. "Is this the appetizer?" he added.

In the small universe that was the Detroit private investigative community, Cade Vance and his firm were considered the top of the heap. He was a white guy, with yellowish hair combed straight back, a handsome face, on a large, very fit frame. He looked like an anchorman or an ex-athlete. His company, Vance Investigations had a bunch of employees and all kinds of departments, including cybercrime. He'd asked me once to join him, but I declined.

I'd sort of lost my appetite seeing him, but I ate the rest of my second burger in two bites and then daintily sipped some coffee.

"What's new, Cade?" I asked. He was dressed in blue jeans, cowboy boots and some kind of linen sport coat. Aviator sunglasses were slid back on his head.

"News of you is new," he said.

"Oh yeah?"

"Mmhmm. Rumor is you were somehow involved with that girl who was murdered and made into some kind of fucked-up art piece."

I shrugged, which made him laugh.

"You're not just a closed book," he said. "You're a book that someone closed and covered with super glue."

"Why are you so interested?" I asked.

"I just heard it was a really bad scene. Was the girl a client?"

"I'm afraid that's privileged information," I said.

Carla came over and Cade ordered a coffee and a slice of pie.

"Look, I can help you. I've got a whole team that could–"

"I'm not working the case," I told him. "She wasn't my client."

He nodded, as if he'd known that all along. I hadn't exactly lied. I wasn't working the case, I was just poking around, kind of like a pro bono thing.

Carla came over to refill my water and I reached for my wallet.

"No, I got this," Cade said. And then to Carla, "Put his tab on mine."

"That's okay," I said, tossing down a bill that was almost double the cost of my lunch.

As I started to walk by, Cade leaned back, blocking my way. "August, I'm telling you this as a friend. Walk away from whatever you're doing with this dead girl thing."

"How about I just walk away now?" I asked.

He leaned forward so I could walk by.

Outside, the sky had gone gray once again.

It perfectly matched my mood.

CHAPTER EIGHT

SMOKE FILLED THE BACK ROOM, along with low voices and the sound of ice hitting the bottom of a glass. Rock music from the main room reverberated through the floor. Heavy red velvet drapes covered most of the walls, their thick folds drawn tightly. The only illumination came from a few scattered lamps, their light softened into a deep amber.

Occasionally, a DJ could be heard announcing the newest dancer.

The place had a single name, Oasis, and was ostensibly a strip club and lounge. It was frequented almost exclusively by people with deep ties to the Middle East.

There was a back room where the dancers

could change, and then another door that led to a secure series of rooms that were part lounge area, part bar and business space. No customers were allowed, and for those who made the mistake of trying, a heavy penalty was paid in the form of a beating or worse.

Currently, a group of men sat in a rough semicircle as a woman wearing only a thin veil and stiletto heels danced before them. She was erratic and her eyes were wild. Whatever drugs were running through her veins they were doing their job.

Two of the men had cigars, all of them had whiskey.

"To us," one of them said and they all raised their glasses.

Everyone but Jibril.

Another woman wearing nothing but a G-string and clear acrylic heels walked into the room and sat on the lap of the biggest man in the room.

"Jibril, I heard you were looking for me," she said.

The big man ignored her.

He wore olive green pants and a dark shirt over his broad shoulders and muscular frame. His hands, large and powerful, and a half-finished cigar was held loosely between the fingers of his right hand, a thin trail of smoke rising from its tip.

He set the cigar down on a crystal ashtray, the glowing embers casting a faint red light that flickered in the darkness.

Jibril's voice, when he finally spoke, was low and steady.

"Out," he said.

Immediately, both women left the room. The other men leaned in to hear what Jibril had to say.

"This is not a celebration."

No one challenged him.

"A score was settled but we are not finished," he said.

He turned to a small wiry man. "What did Malik say?"

"A man came into the store and showed a picture of her. Asked if he'd seen her around. It seemed like the man didn't know her. Malik said it was clear the man did not know she was dead."

Jibril said nothing. He took a drag from his cigar, blew it out, and chased it with a sip of whiskey.

This time, he turned to a different man.

"And the police?"

"Getting nowhere," he answered.

"Still investigating?"

The man nodded.

"That is not good."

"No," the man admitted. "They have a woman. A black detective. Her name is Monroe. The word is that she is… how you say… tenacious."

Another man added, "They'll never figure out who killed Hala. But the investigation could lead to other areas. Areas we don't want the police looking into."

No one said anything for several minutes.

"Put men on the cop and the guy asking questions. For now, just watch them."

Jibril stood, indicating the meeting was over. The men filed out and the woman who had perched herself on the big man's lap entered the room.

She walked up to him and he slapped her, a hard vicious blow that momentarily knocked her unconscious.

"Never interrupt," he said. She got to her feet and Jibril grabbed her by the throat and dragged her into a back room outfitted with a bed.

The door, black encased in red velvet, closed and locked.

PART THREE

CHAPTER NINE

THE DETROIT POLICE DEPARTMENT had moved from a beautiful old building on Beaumont to the Detroit Public Safe Center. A new, contemporary tower of glass with multiple shards and bevels.

Inside, the lobby was vast and institutional. Civilians waited on hard plastic chairs, their faces a mix of anxiety and boredom. Some fidgeted nervously, while others stared blankly at their phones or the informational posters that lined the walls. The posters, faded and curling at the edges, spoke of crime prevention and community outreach programs.

Eventually, I found my way to the reception desk.

As I approached the front desk, I took in the bulletproof glass and marveled at how thick it was. I wondered what was the highest caliber weapon it could withstand.

Behind the glass, an officer sat, his attention focused on the paperwork before him. He was an older guy with a pair of readers perched on his nose. He peered at me over their clear frames.

"I'm here to see Detective Monroe," I said.

He glanced down at a long sheet with names and times.

"Your name?"

"August High."

He peered at me over the frames. "Everyone who comes in here seems to be high."

I smiled out of politeness.

"Okay, driver's license."

After handing it to him, he looked up and said, "That really is your name."

"Yes."

Without a word, he pushed a sign-in sheet towards me through the small opening at the bottom of the glass partition.

Using a pen attached to the counter by a thin chain, I signed my name on the log.

After signing, the officer handed me a temporary ID badge through the same opening. The plastic was slightly warm, as if it had just been printed. "Third floor," the officer said. He pointed towards the elevator bank on the far side of the lobby.

With the visitor badge now clipped to my jacket I made my way to the elevators. The doors opened with a soft ding, revealing a large interior with scuffed metal walls. Two uniformed officers joined me and the air in the elevator was thick with the officers' cologne along with the faint smell of gun oil and leather from the officers' gear.

The homicide unit was a large, open area with two rows of cubicles down the middle, and offices on either side. The space was filled with the sounds of ringing phones, hurried conversations, and the constant hum of computer equipment.

Desks were cluttered with case files, photographs, and paperwork. Post-it notes in various colors adorned computer monitors. Coffee cups in various states of emptiness littered the workspaces. There was the occasional Lions mini helmet or Tigers cap, but no sign of Pistons gear. Not surprising, they were terrible this year.

Detective Monroe stepped out of one of the offices and waved me over. As I walked past the cubicles, a few heads popped and watched. I was used to it. Men of my size were rare. Ones with my beat-up face and scarred hands even more so.

Monroe turned and I followed her into the office. Today, she had on a black leather skirt and short suit jacket with a white blouse. She looked good.

"You do attract attention, don't you?" she asked. Looking around her office, I saw no photos of kids, or a husband. Just some professional citations, a calendar and various index cards of multiple colors with words and numbers that made no sense to me. Reference books were stacked on shelves lining one wall, their spines bearing titles related to forensics, criminal psychology, and law enforcement procedures. A small window would have provided a view but that possibility was prevented by a set of thick venetian blinds.

My gaze returned to her. "Yeah, like an elephant at the circus."

"More like the strong man," she said.

I just shrugged my shoulders.

"Let's talk about Hala Yousef," she said.

"Okay."

"Take me through your involvement one more time."

I did as she asked, my story not changing one molecule from the two times I'd already told it.

As I spoke, Monroe listened but I didn't think she really cared. That wasn't why she'd called me down for an interview. No, something else was going on. I just had to let her find her way at her own pace.

She jotted down notes in a small notebook and occasionally she would nod or make a small sound of acknowledgment, encouraging me to continue.

When I finished my account, Monroe looked up from her notes.

"And since that night, have you learned anything about the victim?"

Ah, there we were. She wanted to know if I was snooping around her investigation.

I met her gaze and decided to tell the truth. "I visited her studio, that's about it."

Monroe almost flinched but caught it at the last moment.

The cops didn't know about the studio.

"Do you want the address?" I asked, trying not to sound like a smart ass, but I'm pretty sure that's how it came off. From her desk I snatched a pen and jotted it down on an index card and pushed it across to her.

She seemed to apprise me differently. "I was expecting you to stonewall."

"Not my style," I replied. "Unless someone gives me a reason to, and you haven't."

With a nod, she slid the index card into her notebook.

"Are you going to keep nosing around?" she asked.

"Probably not since I don't have a paying client and the rent is due the first of every month."

Her looks said she didn't really believe me and I didn't expect her to. The truth was, I didn't know where this thing was going.

"How about you?" I asked. "How's it going?"

"Not much," she said. "This is confidential, of course."

"Okay."

"About all we've learned is that she has a few extended family members in the area and they all said Hala had a drug problem and they always figured someone from that life might do her in."

Monroe didn't believe that, and neither did I.

"Do me a favor?" she asked.

I lowered my head, wondering what she was going to ask.

"I haven't interviewed Jazz Park. She's working tonight at The Twelve. I'd appreciate if you could join me. She might be more talkative with you there."

"Hey, any reason to go to a bar is good by me. What time?"

"Eight-ish."

"Okay."

She turned back to her computer and I walked through Cubicle Land again where I endured the same gawkers.

Outside, I walked to the Maverick feeling pretty good.

Detective Monroe had just asked me out on a date.

CHAPTER TEN

MY OLD STOMPING GROUNDS. Really, my first stomping grounds.

From Detroit's police headquarters, I made my way to an old, forgotten building along the Detroit River. Not on the water, mind you, but two blocks off.

I parked the Maverick almost a block away, noting that most of the parking spaces right in front of the old place were taken.

Good for him, I thought.

There was no sign. There never had been.

I heaved open the heavy metal door and stepped into the place where I'd been raised. It was a boxing gym, dominated by a ring in the center, and around the outskirts, heavy bags and speed bags and jump ropes and weights along with some treadmills and exercise bikes.

There was a pretty intense sparring match going on, which I watched for a few minutes.

The walls were adorned with vintage boxing posters, and the ring in the center of the room had seen countless rounds of practice. The air was thick with the smell of leather and sweat, mixed with a faint hint of liniment oil.

I spotted Earl "Pops" Walker near the back of the gym. Pops was an ancient black man with a commanding presence despite his frail physique. He was peering intently at the ring.

A few other men were around him, waiting for his thoughts.

"He's telegraphing his right," Pops growled. His voice sounded like an old soup can being dragged across a rusty washboard. His face, etched with deep lines, was set in a look of concentration.

Without looking over at me he said, "I should put August in there just for fun."

I glanced over at the ring. *Not a bad idea*, I thought.

Again, without even looking at me or the men around him he said, "I adopted that big brute from an orphanage. I went in and said give me the biggest, meanest, ugliest baby you got." Now he looked at me. "And here he is."

The other men chuckled, they'd heard the story and joke many times. I had too, but it always made me laugh. Mostly because I know it was one hundred percent true.

We waited for the fight to end and Pops told the men what they needed to work on with their fighter. Afterward, he looked at me.

"Let's go to my office."

Pops struggled to his feet and I was tempted to reach out to help him but I knew he hated that and would bark at me. So I waited, tense, ready to catch him if he fell.

But he didn't.

Slowly, we made our way to his office. There was a big old oak desk, an ancient swivel chair, and the walls were covered with fight posters. It always brought back so many memories. Just down from the office were living quarters, where Pops lived. I had my own room when I was growing up. Pops had his, and he shared it with an ever-evolving group of ladies. They all liked me and were nice to me.

He dropped into his chair.

"Where's Sheila?" I asked. In need of a part-time caregiver, I hired a retired nurse I knew and had her keep an eye on the old man for me. He was a handful.

"Went to the pharmacy, I guess, for more pills. That's all I do these days."

"Modern medicine is amazing," I replied. "Embrace it."

"Yeah right. Did you see those fighters out there? Where's the fire? No one's got the fire anymore."

He narrowed his eyes at me. "You still do, though. You'll never lose it."

I wasn't so sure but I appreciated the compliment.

"So what brings you in?" he asked.

"I was visiting someone nearby, just wanted to see if you were up in the ring trying to relive your glory days."

Pops had been a legendary boxer, a flyweight, with the deadly combination of speed and power. A punch that tore apart the retina in his left eye did in his career.

In very vague terms I told him about Holla, but just described her as an artist who'd been killed and I was looking into it for the family. Pops acted tough, but deep down he was a tender soul. Describing what I'd seen in the warehouse would probably make him lose sleep for a week.

There was a knock at the door and Pops said, "Sheila, it's open."

He looked at me. "She's the only one whoever knocks."

The nurse walked in, a strong and capable woman with a kind face and a no-nonsense way of talking. Perfect for the old man.

"You're taking good care of him," I said. "Glad you know how to handle the mean ones."

She laughed. "Oh yeah. You think he's a tough old bird but he's as sweet as a little baby poodle."

This time I laughed and Pops glowered at both of us.

"Visiting hours are over," he said.

I got to my feet and said, "I'll be by next week."

As I exited the building and headed for my car, I spotted Gretchen Mercer standing in my way. The intrepid journalist was on me again.

"So I heard you paid a visit to Pulse," she said.

It took me a moment to remember the arrogant artist whose bodyguard I'd knocked senseless.

"Yeah, I was interested in buying a sculpture."

She laughed. "Like you could afford one. Don't get me wrong, I couldn't either."

"So?" I asked. I was going to give her five seconds before I moved her out of the way.

"Hala Yousef," she said. "What do you know?"

"Nothing."

"Come on," she whined. "If Pulse had anything to do with her murder, it would rock this city. National news would be all over it, too."

"You'd be famous," I replied.

Gretchen glared at me. "I'm a reporter. Not a social media star."

Finally, just to get rid of her I said, "You have a card?"

She leaned back to see if I was serious.

"I'll help you out, so one day, you can help me," I said. "If I need it. Which I doubt I will."

"You got it."

"Have someone show you her studio in Ferndale," I replied.

Her mouth dropped open.

"Better hurry, though. I believe the cops are on their way, too."

She dashed off and I climbed back into the Maverick. As I drove away, I could see her in the rearview mirror, driving like a mad woman.

CHAPTER
ELEVEN

AFTER LEAVING THE GYM, I got back into my Maverick and started driving toward my loft. The streets of Detroit were a mix of the familiar and the forgotten—old brick buildings with faded signs, cracked sidewalks, and the occasional neon light flickering above a corner store. The sun was beginning to set, casting long shadows across the pavement.

After settling into the drive and putting my cell on speaker, I asked it to dial Paul Fawcett's number. Paul, the former cop turned tech expert, was always my go-to when it came to digging up information or analyzing data I couldn't make sense of.

The phone rang a few times before Paul's voice came through. "High. You're still alive."

"Alive and kicking."

"You're probably calling about that piece of paper."

"That and something else."

I heard him clap his hands together. "Now we're talking. So I've got good news and bad news."

"Give me the bad. Always start with the bad."

He laughed. "That's how I am too," he said. "The bad news is the blood had soaked through the ink and the paper was basically ruined. I was not able to make out any word."

"Okay."

"The good news is I don't believe the message was a word. I believe the entire note consisted of only three letters."

"Three letters?"

"Yeah. I'm also positive the first is an A. The second is really impossible to decipher. It could be an I, a T, or an L, and maybe even a lowercase D. And I'm fairly certain the last letter is an M. But that, too could be a V or maybe a W. But my best guess is M."

"Is it a name? Or an abbreviation? Aim.

ATM. Alm. What's an alm? Isn't something religious?"

"Look at you," he said. "Just a regular Bible scholar. You're thinking of almsgiving, which is basically participating in charity for those less fortunate."

I considered the other option. "Could it be just a reminder that she needed to go to the ATM? But I'm almost certain she swallowed the paper just before she died. Why would you want to hide a note about going to the ATM?"

"No idea," Paul said. "I'll keep the note and maybe run a few artificial intelligence programs, but I don't think it will amount to much. What else you got?"

I had been thinking about the paintings of the dead men in Hala's studio. "Can you run a check on any recent killings of men? Murder, especially. And even better, if they were mutilated in some way. There's been nothing in the news or gossip about something like that, so I'm thinking they might be John Does."

"But you don't know if there are actually any at all, right?"

"Yeah, it's a guess based on some really

weird shit."

"You got it," Paul said. "Stop by some time for dinner. Found a great take-out joint with phenomenal Pad Thai."

"Deal," I said.

We disconnected from the call and thought about the letters. Holla was an artist. It could have just been a design. Who knew with modern art these days? Maybe she swallowed the paper and then was going to frame it and sell it for a few grand.

It seemed preposterous but my line of thought was broken when a white SUV appeared in my rearview mirror. Again. I'd seen the damn thing three times already, even after some pretty major shifts in direction.

It was time to be a little more aggressive. I took a few turns faster than usual but the SUV mirrored my every move. On the next street, with a wide-open lane and no lights, I stomped on the accelerator like I was squashing a bug. The Maverick, sporting a beast of a V8 under the hood, shot forward. No way the guy could keep up. When there was nearly a quarter mile between us, I threw the car into a vicious left turn, followed by two more before I rocketed back on to the street where we'd just been.

Ahead, the SUV took the same left and I followed, gaining on them quickly. We continued on for a few blocks and I was impressed. The driver must have seen me behind him by now but he stayed cool. I wished the vehicle in front of me didn't have tinted windows. There was no way to see who was inside.

Suddenly, the SUV belched black smoke and surged forward. Their vehicle was no match for mine, though, and no distance was gained.

They must have realized that, too, because the rear window, also tinted, rolled down just enough for someone to stick a gun out and point it right at me. I saw flame shoot from the muzzle and I pushed the Maverick to the right. The sound of bullets ricocheting off pavement reached my ears and then something hit my car like a rock. But I knew it was a bullet.

The SUV managed to slip into a narrow alley and I had no desire to follow. If they had a second car, they could trap me in the middle and open up a shooting gallery.

I skidded to a stop at the alley's entrance, watching as the SUV disappeared into the city's backstreets. I could hear the fading roar of its engine, and knew they were gone.

Exiting the Maverick, I found the bullet hole. It was in the front bumper on the right, and it had glanced off. No damage.

Well, someone knew I was investigating, and they wanted to send a message.

The problem with sending one, is that you'll most likely get a return message.

And mine tended to be very impactful.

CHAPTER
TWELVE

THERE WAS nothing like a wild car chase through Detroit featuring gunshots to make a man long for a drink.

The Twelve was, as always, a welcome respite, no matter what was going on, or what kind of day I'd had. I parked the car and walked up to the entrance, the muffled strains of blues music reaching my ears. Inside, the bar was as it always was—dimly lit, with the smell of bourbon and smoke hanging in the air and the sound of good blues music everywhere.

The usual crowd was there, regulars nursing drinks and chatting quietly. In one corner, a musician was setting up for the night's set, the soft tuning of his guitar blending with the low murmur of conversation.

Detective Monroe was already at the bar, seated on one of the tall chairs with a martini in hand. She was dressed in a simple, sharp outfit, her posture relaxed as she listened to a man who was talking animatedly beside her. The guy was leaning in close, clearly trying to make an impression.

There was an empty seat next to Monroe, so I took it. The man talking to her glanced at me, his expression shifting the moment he got a good look. He hesitated, then mumbled something about needing to take a call. As he fumbled with his phone and hurriedly walked away, Monroe turned to me, a small smile tugging at the corner of her lips.

"Remind me to call you when I need a room cleared."

"My pleasure," I said.

The bartender placed a whiskey in front of me. I raised my glass and softly clinked it against Monroe's martini glass.

We both nodded and sipped.

Jazz Park was working behind the bar. She caught sight of me and Monroe, gave a quick nod, and then continued with her work. It wasn't long before she finished what she was doing and made her way over to us.

"August," she said to me and then to Monroe, "I assume you're Detective Monroe?"

"You are correct."

"It's time for my break if you want to chat."

"Sounds good," Monroe replied.

Jazz motioned for us to follow her as she led us to an area in back, much quieter than the bar. Monroe and I brought our drinks, and Jazz had grabbed a beer.

"Tell me how you came to know Hala, and the night you recommended she contact August."

Jazz went through the exact same thing she had told me. Monroe asked a few questions, almost exactly the same ones I had, and received the exact same answers. Which basically amounted to not much.

She must have seen the slight frustration because she added, "However, I've been thinking about Hala since the last time we talked," she said to me. "There's something I remembered after you left."

I took a sip of my whiskey, indicating she should continue.

"I only served her once or twice, but I remember one time she'd ordered an unusual drink. It might have been a Sazerac or something. When she sipped it, she was shocked at the taste and the strength and she mumbled a little joke. I wasn't even sure what she had said."

"What do you think she said, Jazz?" I asked.

"Well, for sure, she said something like, 'Boy you can't get this in…'"

Monroe said, "In… where?"

"At first, I thought she said something like baccarat. You know, the casino game. But later, I realized that didn't really make sense and I decided she hadn't included a T at the end of the word."

"Bacarah," Monroe said.

Jazz nodded. "A few days later, when I was bored and wasting time on my phone, I decided to google it. A bunch of nonsense came up, but then there was an entry for Bacarah." She spelled it out for us.

Both Monroe and I had our phones, but we waited for Jazz to finish the story.

"What did you find?" I asked.

"Considering her name, I figured I had gotten it right."

She looked at me.

"Bacarah is a small village."

Jazz sipped her beer.

"A small village where?" Monroe asked.

"In Iraq."

It had gotten late and I was on my third whiskey, Monroe her second martini.

"Do you live around here?" she suddenly asked me.

"Yeah, a few blocks away."

That information seemed to register with her.

"Want to see it?" I asked. "You know, we could talk about the case some more. Spitball a little bit."

Monroe made a show of checking her watch.

"Maybe a quick nightcap," she said. We left and she followed me back to my loft. This time, with her, I used the elevator instead of the stairs.

When she walked into my apartment she smiled and said, "This is exactly what I thought it would look like."

I laughed and said, "What's your place like?"

"A duplex on Adams in Indian Village. 11A if you ever want to drop by."

"You want something to drink?"

"No."

Monroe had gone over to my workout area and she pushed the heavy bag. It barely moved. "Is this where you do all of your exercising?"

"Yeah."

She pointed over toward the open door of my bedroom. "Not in there?"

I walked up to her. "Only if I have a partner who can spot me."

Monroe walked into my arms and our lips met. It was a solid kiss, full of potential. She put her hands on my chest and slid them over my shoulders and then she pushed me back toward the bedroom.

"Let's see how many reps we can get in before I have to go," she said.

If you're curious, the number was four.

PART FOUR

CHAPTER
THIRTEEN

THE NEXT DAY, with memories of the delicious havoc that occurred between the sheets with Monroe, I navigated my way to a halfway house on the near east side. Along the way, there were dozens of abandoned buildings, open parks overgrown with weeds and an occasional house that was neat and tidy and obviously occupied. You had to admire them for sticking it out when all around them was like a set in an apocalyptic movie.

The facility where my friend Sam Hopkins was staying fit right in; a low, squat building that seemed to hunker down against the relentless decay surrounding it. Its gray exterior blended seamlessly into the overcast day, the atmosphere heavy with overcast clouds threatening rain. The rusting chain-link fence surrounding it offered more of a suggestion of security than any real protection, the twisted metal jutting out like rusted-out thorns.

I'd known him before he'd gone off to fight various wars, mostly in Iraq. When he came back, he wasn't the Sam I knew.

That happened to a lot of guys, and like many before him, my friend found solace from the battlefield nightmares in drugs and booze. For years he was a lost soul but then he finally got clean.

Coming to see him felt wrong. Because of what I was going to ask him to do.

With some trepidation I parked the Maverick outside the facility and locked it. There was a security guard at the entrance to the place who might prevent the car being stolen. Then again, he might call someone and let them know a big white guy had been dumb enough to park his car and leave it in the hood.

Past the security guard I found myself facing an attendant who looked like she'd rather be anywhere else; her eyes were glazed over, her expression flat as she glanced up at me from behind a thick pane of glass.

"I'm here to see Sam Hopkins," I said.

The attendant nodded without much interest, running a finger down a clipboard until she found the right line. She checked my ID, wrote down my name and then buzzed me in, the metal door clicking open with a thick, clunky sound.

Inside, the place was as drab as I'd expected. The walls were a dull, institutional beige, the kind of color that saps your energy rather than revives it. The floors were covered in cheap linoleum that had seen better days, scraped to hell and worn from the countless feet that had trudged through these halls. A faint smell of disinfectant hung in the air, mingling with the underlying scent of despair.

A few men were scattered around the common area, their attention fixed on a television. It looked like a reality show: people surviving on an island while trying to get rid of the others.

How appropriate, I thought.

I'd come to see Sam before, when he'd first landed here. Depending on the individual resident's status, visiting typically took place in a small room where I found Sam waiting.

He was sitting at a table, hunched over slightly, his broad shoulders slumping as he cradled a paper cup of coffee in his hands. The steam curled upwards and when he looked up and saw me, a tired smile broke through the lines on his face, but it didn't quite reach his eyes; those were still filled with shadows that had yet to retreat.

"August," he said, standing up to shake my hand. His grip was strong. He was a good-looking guy, square jaw, with light-colored hair and a few tattoos here and there.

"Good to see you, man," I replied, taking the seat across from him. The room was sparsely furnished—just the table and a couple of chairs, with a small window that let in a sliver of the dull light outside.

"How's it going?" I asked, more out of habit than expectation. We both knew the answer; life didn't really have a "going" when you were inside a halfway house.

Sam shrugged, running a hand through

his short-cropped hair, the action a familiar gesture that felt almost soothing. "One day at a time, you know how it is."

"Yeah," I said.

We made small talk for a while about some of the wacky stuff he'd seen in the place so far, and Detroit sports teams and a few other friends we had vaguely in common.

Finally, he said, "So what brings you here?"

I leaned forward slightly, not feeling great about what I had to ask. It would require him to think back to things I knew he'd had trouble dealing with.

"I'm looking into a situation that might have some connections to Iraq. You ever hear of a village called Bacarah?"

He squinted his eyes. "Hmm. You know, they all started to sound alike after all. No, I don't think so. Doesn't really ring a bell. What part of Iraq is it?"

"Somewhere in the north," I replied, having looked it up.

"Tons of drugs up there, especially if it's near Syria."

"That makes sense," I thought. Monroe

had mentioned Hala's family thought she was having drug issues.

"You know, a lot of them wound up here."

"Who?"

"The drug runners. They poured into Dearborn after most of the wars had settled down. And not just them," he said. "Former Iraq special ops guys left, too. Not to mention the local militia we gave millions of dollars to for basically nothing. Most of our guys came back broke and broken, the Iraqis arrived in America flush, ready to invest and make even more."

I did know that.

"They love car washes and laundromats and convenience stores. Lots of cash for laundering purposes."

That was also a well-known fact.

Finally, he said, "Why?"

Careful not to drag him back into things he'd struggled to forget I said, "A young woman was killed and she was apparently from Bacarah. It doesn't feel like an ordinary murder to me. This was something else and I'm trying to figure out what that might be."

He nodded. "I know a few guys who were up in northern Iraq, near Mosul. I can ask them about Bacarah." He held up an iPhone. "Cell phones are no longer off-limits. Here, I'll text you my number."

My phone buzzed with the message.

"Do you need anything?" I asked.

Sam shook his head. I slid a small envelope across the table to him. "This is my payment up front."

"Payment for what?"

"You're on my payroll now, helping me with a case. Don't worry, I'll mark it up and bill my client for it," I said with a laugh.

He didn't look inside. His eyes met mine and he said, "I appreciate it, August."

As I turned to go, Sam stopped me.

"I never worry about you, August. But be careful on this one. If you're getting involved with these guys, they're not the kind you want to underestimate. They don't play by the same rules as anyone else. They play by no rules. And they think America is a weak country where they can literally do whatever they want. That includes killing nosy private investigators."

"I'll keep that in mind."

The men in the common area barely glanced up as I passed, their attention still fixated on the TV. Outside, I was relieved to see the Maverick still there, on its own tires and not up on blocks.

It seemed to me like everyone was warning me and telling me to be careful.

A guy could get a complex.

CHAPTER
FOURTEEN

THE SUN HUNG low in the sky as I drove through the winding streets of Detroit, the Maverick's engine growling like a feral dog.

My phone buzzed on the passenger seat, vibrating against the worn leather. I glanced at the screen and saw it was Paul. I tapped the speaker button, keeping one hand on the wheel.

"High," Paul's voice crackled through the car speakers, the usual mix of sarcasm and seriousness present. "Got something for you. You might want to head down to the morgue."

I frowned, keeping my eyes on the road. "The morgue?"

"Remember you wanted me to see if there

were any recent John Does, maybe killed and tortured?"

"Yeah."

"Well, there is a pair down at the city morgue. I'm not sure if they were tortured, but from what I heard secondhand, they were both pretty messy kills."

"Got it," I said. "I'm not far away. Did you-"

"Yeah, I told them you might be coming and that it was off the record. Carole is an old friend of mine," he said. I had met Carole Jennings, the city medical examiner, once or twice. She was a straight shooter.

The drive was short, the streets thinning out as I approached the Wayne County Medical Examiner's Office. The brick building looked as cold and unwelcoming as the work done inside. I parked the car and walked up to the entrance, the automatic doors sliding open with a hiss.

Inside, the air was sterile, carrying a faint smell of antiseptic. The receptionist barely glanced up as I approached, her expression indifferent.

"August High," I said, showing my ID. "I'm here to look at two John Does. They should be in the system. I believe Dr. Jennings knew I was coming."

The receptionist typed something into her computer, her fingers moving rapidly across the keyboard. After a moment, she nodded. "You're clear. Room 3. Someone will meet you there."

The hallway was narrow with the kind of quiet that felt heavy, like it had soaked into the walls over the years. It was an eerie silence, totally unlike a library. Maybe it was because most of the people inside were dead.

I found Room 3 easily enough—plain white walls, a metal door with a small window, and the number stenciled on the glass. With a quick knock I opened the door and stepped inside where a woman looked up and waved me over.

She was a tall woman, older than me and she had on white scrubs with green gloves. A face mask hung from her ears and it rested just below her chin.

"Mr. High," she said, her tone professional. "Paul said you'd be stopping by."

"Thanks for meeting with me," I said. And then added, "Unofficially."

"How is Paul?"

"Great. Keeping busy as an investigator and earning a reputation as one of the best in the city. He might be busier than when he had a day job."

She laughed. "I understand you're here to see the John Does."

"That's right," I said. The air inside the room was cold, the temperature controlled to keep the bodies from decomposing too quickly. The room was lined with metal drawers, each one marked with a number. In the center of the room, two bodies lay on gurneys, covered with white sheets.

Dr. Jennings pulled back the sheets, revealing the two men. They were both around the same age, somewhere between the late twenties and mid-thirties. They were both dark-complected, and both had facial hair. One had a mustache and goatee, the other a beard. Their bodies were covered with stab wounds and great slashing cuts across their torsos.

"No ID, no fingerprints in the system," Jennings said. "They both were sent here because of the similarities. They were found in different parts of the city, but there's no doubt they were connected. Same tattoos, same cause of death—a single gunshot wound to the head from most likely a high caliber rifle. The rest of the damage was done post-mortem."

"So maybe they were shot sniper style, and then someone moved in to do this dirty work."

On both of their chests, over their hearts, was a tattoo.

It had three letters: ALM enclosed in a pair of dark wings.

ALM.

Holy shit, I thought. The note in Hala's guts. The one she ate.

"Recognize something?" Jennings asked.

"Maybe," I replied. My thoughts flashed back to what Sam Hopkins had told me earlier—about drug gangs from Iraq now plying their trade in Detroit.

I thanked Dr. Jennings profusely and told her I would give her best to Paul. Once outside and back in the Maverick, I called Sam Hopkins.

He answered on the first ring. "Hey, I was just about to call you," he said. "But you go first."

"Ever hear of a group called ALM? Might be a gang from Iraq?"

There was silence as he thought. "No, but there were so many militias from so many different regions, people tended to abbreviate their names or their homeland."

"Okay," I said. "Your turn."

"I asked around about Bacarah and the general consensus seems to be the guy you want to talk to is Lee Robson. Here's his address. My phone buzzed again. Supposedly, he spent all of his time in that area and if anyone knows the village, he will."

Finally, a solid lead. "Okay, thank you, Sam."

"No problem."

"And Sam?"

"Yeah?"

"I'm always on the lookout for capable people who can lend me a hand now and then. Look me up when you're out, okay?"

"Roger that."

CHAPTER
FIFTEEN

SITTING in the Maverick outside a nondescript house on Detroit's east side, I selected the images from my phone that Dr. Jennings had allowed me to take. That was a very unusual breach of protocol and it told me how much she liked Paul Fawcett.

The two images were attached to a text message I sent to Paul, asking him to look into ALM and see if he could find any information about militias, mercenaries or security firms from Iraq that might bear those letters.

I slid the phone into my pocket, got out of the Maverick and locked it up.

The address was right and I climbed the concrete steps to the front door. It was a very humble Cape Cod style house with window trim that sported peeling paint, and a yard of mostly weeds.

It was a little surprising; most former military guys were neat and orderly.

There was a brass knocker on the door which I used to announce my arrival. There was a doorbell, too, which I pressed but there was no corresponding sound from inside.

I waited, and then tried the knocker again.

There was no car in the driveway and there was no garage.

With a quick check for anyone who might be watching, I tested the doorknob, half-expecting it to be locked, but it turned easily in my hand. The door creaked open, revealing a dimly lit foyer. The smell hit me first and it was unmistakable. I closed the door behind me and drew my .45.

The floor was covered in a threadbare green carpet that muffled my footsteps.

The living room was small and sparsely furnished, with a worn couch, a coffee table covered in old newspapers, and a TV that looked like it hadn't been turned on in months.

To the left was a small kitchen, empty, and a bathroom. Just beyond the living room was a tiny office, not much bigger than a closet. It consisted of an empty desk and an old, beat-up office chair. It had a closet with a filing cabinet, but it was empty, too.

The home was small and I took the stairs to the second floor. A tiny landing met me at the top, with one bedroom on each side. The bedroom on the right was empty, as was the small closet.

The door to the other bedroom was closed.

I opened it.

And found Lee Robson.

He was naked and he'd been nailed to the wall and disemboweled. His eyes were open, staring blankly ahead as if he'd died looking for a way out.

The smell was overwhelming and I covered my nose as best I could. Inside the room I looked for any evidence but found nothing except for a pair of gym shorts and a T-shirt. Whoever killed Robson had surprised him in his sleep. The closet was empty and I went back downstairs.

I opened the kitchen cabinets and it looked like stuff had been tossed around, as if someone had previously searched the place.

Something was missing, though. Every

soldier I knew had a place for their weapons. Even if Robson's killers had cleaned out the place, the weapons probably hadn't been sitting on a shelf or under a bed.

The office.

I went back to the tiny room and once again looked at the empty desk, the shitty chair and the empty file cabinet. This place probably wouldn't have merited much attention from the killer or killers.

The walls of the closet were solid as I gently pounded them with my fist. The same for the room itself. I looked up at the ceiling. It was ceiling tiles, grimy and water stained. It was easy for me to reach without standing on anything and I gently pushed on each tile.

When I got to the second one from the corner I stopped. Just on the edge of the tile I saw the slightest smudge in the grime.

A fingertip.

Someone had recently touched that specific tile. I pushed and it popped upward easily. I had to stand on my tiptoes to feel around but my fingers brushed up against a cardboard box. I pulled it over and it barely fit through the open space in the ceiling.

I took it over to the table and opened it up.

There were two handguns, small automatics that probably would have been used as a back-up option. Along with a box of ammo, there was a photo and a thin deck of playing cards and some papers.

I scooped up the cards and looked at them. There were seven in all. Each card had a man's face on it, like the decks the U.S. military had used during the Iraq War to identify high-value targets. Two of the cards had red lines slashed through them and I recognized the faces immediately.

They were the John Does I'd just seen in the morgue, the ones with the ALM tattoos. They currently didn't look as good as their portraits on the cards.

On each of the remaining five cards was a photo of a man staring back at me with a hostile intensity. I didn't know who these men were, but if they were on these cards, then someone had included them in the deck for a reason.

I pocketed the cards and looked at the photo.

It was of a couple, standing in what looked like a small village in the desert.

The man I had just seen on the bedroom wall.

The woman I had seen recently as well, she'd been hung from a ceiling.

Lee Robson and Hala Yousef. The story told itself: they met in Iraq, fell in love and eventually found each other in Detroit.

The village from the photo was probably Bacarah

And as far as the two men on the playing cards with red marks drawn through them, I had a theory, too.

Robson and Holla had murdered them.

CHAPTER
SIXTEEN

MEET me at the old school near the warehouse where we found Holla. Hurry!

The text from Monroe flashed on my phone just as I was leaving Robson's apartment, the images of the playing cards still fresh in my mind.

Entirely capable of following orders, I cranked up the Maverick and it roared to life as I gunned it for the freeway. Figuring Monroe could get me out of a speeding ticket since I was hurrying on her behalf, I let the big V-8 loose. The car was like a missile, blowing past other cars like they were in slow motion.

In less than fifteen minutes, I put the vehicle's huge brakes to use as I braked hard for my exit. Rounding the corner with the tires screaming in protest, I raced into the same section of town where this whole case had started.

The abandoned school was known to most people. It was a beautiful structure, built in the early twentieth century, but it had been abandoned for at least fifty years. All the windows were broken out and the doors were locked with heavy chains and padlocks. But getting in was easy. The homeless did it all the time, along with drug users and drug dealers.

The school loomed ahead, like the skeleton of a once beautiful and impressive animal. The parking lot was cracked and overgrown, but I spotted Monroe's police car near the entrance. The door to the building was ajar, police tape fluttering in the warm breeze like a tattered flag of surrender.

I parked the car, slid out, and ran toward the door, pushing it open wider and then I was inside the school's main lobby. There was junk everywhere, piles of broken bookcases, pipes, and swaths of insulation tossed about with no rhyme or reason. The walls were lined with old lockers, most of them rusted shut, and the floor was littered with debris. I moved deeper into the darkness.

"Monroe?" I called out.

I had the .45 in my hand and maneuvered my way around a set of gymnasium bleachers that looked like they'd been tipped over–

The slightest scuffle.

A whisper almost.

Just behind me.

I turned to see the blurred motion of a knife as it slashed at my throat. My left hand shot out, catching his elbow as the blade whistled past me. I wrenched the arm and heard the pop of a joint breaking.

My upper shoulder was hit hard and I nearly fell forward. Still holding the first man's broken arm, I wheeled, driving my elbow into his jaw. This time it was less of a pop and more of a horrible cracking sound. I let go and he fell to the ground.

Something just passed by my head and hit a part of the bleacher. Wood shards flew everywhere, some into the back of my neck. I saw the shooter, partially hiding behind a concrete pillar. I waited until he peeked and then I shot him in the face. He flew backward and landed on the marble floor.

A third man came out from the shadows. Too late, I saw what was in his hands: a sawed-off shotgun. I dove for cover just as he fired and pellets tore at my left leg.

I rolled behind a pile of smashed-up wooden desks and heard the man charging. He was determined, I had to give him that. I was now behind a teacher's desk. Big. Heavy.

After ramming my .45 back into my holster, I heaved the desk up and took two steps forward just as the shotgun operator appeared.

He tried to backpedal, but there was nowhere to go. I grabbed his gun hand, squeezing until the bones crunched under the pressure. The gun fell from his grip, clattering to the floor. He tried to pull back, but I was relentless. My fist crashed into his face, breaking his nose with a sickening crunch. Blood sprayed, but I didn't stop. I hit him again, harder this time, and felt his cheekbone shatter.

I knew one of them wasn't dead, and one was all I needed.

This guy was expendable. Rotating fists, I beat his face in until it was nothing like a broken-in catcher's mitt. You couldn't even tell he was human.

I picked up the shotgun and walked over to the first guy. He was still unconscious so I picked up his knife and stabbed him in the groin. His eyes shot open and I put the muzzle of the shotgun into his teeth, breaking a few along the way.

"When I take this shotgun out of your mouth, I want a name, and a location."

Slowly, I withdrew the weapon from his bloody lips.

Barely audible, he whispered a name. And then a second name.

"Very good," I said. And then I blew his head off with three blasts from the shotgun.

"That's for what you did to Holla," I said.

I'd been shot and the pain was radiating through my upper shoulder. I knew no bone was broken, though, because it would have been a lot worse.

I scooped up the pistol from the guy who'd been hiding behind the pillar. It was a Glock, military issue.

Armed with my own pistol, the Glock, the knife and shotgun, I walked out of the building.

My breath was coming rapidly, not from exertion.

The corners of my vision were tinged with crimson.

But beyond the anger and the rage, the cold truth hit me more powerfully than any bullet.

Monroe was dead.

PART FIVE

CHAPTER
SEVENTEEN

INDIAN VILLAGE
On Adams.
11 A.

That's what Monroe had told me the night we spent in my loft. My jaws clenched. *Don't think about it,* I said to myself. *You know what you're going to find.*

I could feel blood dripping from the gunshot wound in my upper back. It was seeping through my shirt, onto the Maverick's leather seat, and running down the side.

The streets were like a blur and the playing cards still in my pocket were giving off a controlled heat. I knew it was in my mind. But those faces were calling. Calling for me to come and destroy them.

The duplex was dark when I arrived, the wide street quiet. I moved quickly, crossing the yard in a few long strides and taking the steps up to the front door two at a time.

The door was solid, a heavy oak slab that had likely withstood decades of weather and time. It was locked, probably did so automatically, but it wasn't going to stop me.

I took a step back, then drove my boot into the wood just above the handle. The doorframe splintered with a sharp crack, the door flying open as the lock gave way.

I stepped inside, gun drawn, and saw a door to my right, and a stairwell to my left. The letter A was marked on the door. The door opened when I turned the handle and I stepped into the apartment. The place was neat, orderly, with just a few personal touches that hinted at Monroe's life outside the badge—pictures on the walls, a small table with a vase of flowers, magazines on a coffee table.

The kitchen was spotless and I saw a recipe tacked to the fridge for a spinach salad.

At the back of the kitchen was a doorway that led into a short hallway. The place smelled like Monroe – perfume and her presence.

A bathroom was on the left and a bedroom on the right where I found her.

She put up a hell of a fight, I thought.

Monroe was lying half on the bed, half off, her body twisted in an unnatural way. The sheets were soaked with blood, dark and thick, staining the white cotton. Gently, I lifted her so she was flat on the bed. Her face was a mess. Swollen and distended, cracked lips, and scratches and cuts. Her arms were torn up as well, and I could see the blood and flesh underneath her nails. Whoever killed her would be wearing some obvious signs.

She'd clearly been shot in the chest several times, and it looked like someone had stabbed her and then thrust the blade upward, slicing through as many vital organs as possible.

I pulled a white sheet over her body and stood still for a moment. She'd been strong, tough, funny and passionate. I wished I'd had the honor of knowing her longer.

A weight sank onto my chest like a heavy stone. Guilt. *I should have been here*, I thought.

I turned away from the bed, went back through the apartment and paused at the door. There would be no coming back.

The gym wasn't far, and I knew Pops would still be there. He always was. And usually, Milt, the trainer stayed last as well.

From my glove compartment, I pulled out a burner cell phone and fired it up, then called 9-1-1 and said there had been gunfire from Monroe's address. It was the least I could do to not prolong the loss of her dignity anymore.

Pops was inside, seated in his usual spot, watching a young fighter working with his trainer. He took one look at me and whistled.

Milt lifted his head from the other side of the ring. He was a tiny guy, Norwegian I think, and he hurried over. Once he saw me, hurried back, grabbed his bag, and gestured toward the office.

Inside the office I said to him, "Never know when you might need a really good cut man."

"Shh," he said. He cut away the part of my shirt covering the gunshot wound.

"Ready?" he asked.

"Yep."

He poured something on the wound and it

burned like a blowtorch. He dug around and pulled out the bullet, dropping it without fanfare onto Pop's desk.

From the bag, Milt took a needle and thread, dousing the wound one more time and then slapping a bandage over it.

"Always in trouble, aren't you?" Pops growled from the doorway.

"You want me to do something about your legs?" Milt asked.

I looked down, having forgotten about the shotgun blast. My pants were torn to shreds and dried blood was everywhere.

"Shit," I said. "No, those pellets will fall out eventually."

I got to my feet and pulled a C-note from my wallet and slipped it into the pocket of Milt's shirt. "Appreciate it, doctor."

"Any time."

"Whatever bullshit you got yourself into, is it over now?" Pops growled at me.

"Sure is," I said as I breezed past him.

Pops gave me a look, the kind of look that said he knew I was full of crap, but he wasn't going to argue. Milt handed me a bottle of painkillers, which I pocketed.

The drive back to my loft was quick, and I

entered with my .45 drawn. My security was ridiculous, but I swept the place anyway. It was clear.

After a quick shower where I picked out most of the shotgun pellets, I put on black pants, black T-shirt, and a bulletproof vest.

Inside the small room I called my armory, a vast array of weapons was on display. Automatic pistols, sound suppressors, hugely powerful revolvers, shotguns and rifles.

I wondered how much I might need.

Probably all of it, I thought.

CHAPTER EIGHTEEN

PAUL ASKED me to stop by, so I showed up, even though it was late. It was fine. For my next step, it was a little too early anyway.

He opened the door, took in what I was wearing, and said, "Jesus. Where's the war?"

For a moment, I almost told him but thought better of it.

Inside, he took a look at me and shook his head. I'd left the bulletproof vest in the car, at least.

"I didn't know they made that shit in your size," he said.

"It's all at the Big & Tall store."

He wheeled himself into his office and I followed, sitting in the chair from which the computer screen was visible.

"Lots to fill you in on," he said. The photos I'd taken of the tattoo on the dead guys in the morgue appeared on the screen. "At first, I couldn't find anything on ALM and believe me, I left no stone unturned. It was only when I added those little wings to the search, that the answer finally appeared."

"What is it?"

"Almalayikat almuntaqamun."

"Come again?"

"It's Arabic for Avenging Angels."

I scoffed. "Yeah. String up innocent girls, kill women. What exactly do they think they're avenging?"

"Who knows?" he asked. "Very little known about them but best guess is they're a quasi-religious paramilitary outfit. Maybe they see themselves as agents of divine retribution or something."

"That's bullshit. The only thing these assholes worship is money. They're running drugs and laundering the money through convenience stores."

I reached into my jacket and pulled out the deck of playing cards I'd found at Robson's place, spreading them out on the table in front of Paul. The cards told the story. Seven men. Two dead. The other three I'd yet to cross off with a red marker. I pushed those three next to the other two dead men.

"Five down, two to go," I said.

Paul glanced at me out of the corner of his eye. "I don't want to know."

We studied the cards. He picked up both of them and peered closely. He flipped them over and set one back on the table. He held up the one in his hand. "Did you see this?" he asked.

"Yeah, never seen him before."

"No, do you see the faded ink on the back?"

I leaned in closer. I still couldn't see it.

Paul held up his glasses. "These are kind of like blue light glasses. Very helpful."

He scanned it and blew up the image on the computer screen.

Now I saw it. Barely.

"Jabril?" I asked, covering my surprise. That was one of the names the dying guy in the abandoned school told me just before I blew his head off. "Is that what it says?"

Paul was typing it into the computer. He

sat back and waited. "Well, that makes sense."

"What does?"

"I translated it. It's Arabic for *Gabriel*."

The name meant nothing to me.

"Think back to the Bible, August."

I shook my head. I must have skipped that Sunday.

"Gabriel is an angel in most religions."

"Here we go again. This guy's a murderer and a drug runner."

"Yeah, but he sees himself as Gabriel?"

"What's the biggest deal with Gabriel, or Jabril."

"He's considered the most powerful and dangerous angel… ever."

"What a load of shit," I said. "Let me tell you my theory. I can't prove it yet but I know someone who can."

"The floor is yours," Paul said.

"Bacarah is a small village in northern Iraq. A U.S. serviceman met a young Iraqi woman named Hala Yousef. He brought her back to the States and they embarked on a mission. The ALM or whatever the hell they are, probably slaughtered, raped and plundered Bacarah. It's possible they killed some or all of Hala Yousef's family."

"Okay, I'm tracking," Paul said.

"Right, so this ALM organization establishes itself here in Detroit, mostly in Dearborn, and join the drug trade, probably with money funded by people on both sides of the war, and with access to plenty of pure product. They use, among other things, convenience stores to sell the stuff, or launder the money, or both."

"Yeah, I've heard about those scams."

"So now, Hala discovers she doesn't have to go back to Iraq to take her vengeance. She decides to start taking out the so-called Avenging Angels right here. She kills two of them with Robson before they get caught and killed themselves."

"It all sounds right," he said. "But you don't have proof."

"Not yet," I admitted. "But do me a favor, see if you can find anything on a massacre in Bacarah. No big deal if you can't. There's a reporter I know, Gretchen Mercer, who's like a pit bull on steroids. Send her everything we have so far. It might take her awhile to connect the dots, but I think she can, eventually."

"Okay." He looked me over. "And I think I know where you're going, am I right?"

The look on my face must have been very unpleasant, because Paul leaned back slightly.

"I'm going to send two angels to Hell."

CHAPTER NINETEEN

OASIS.

It was the other name the now-headless avenging angel had given me.

I'd never heard of it. But a few quick calls told me it was a strip club in Dearborn, popular only with area residents, which was a wink-wink, nudge-nudge that red-blooded Americans probably weren't welcome.

I was ready and dressed for the occasion: all black, with a thick vest beneath a black T-shirt that wouldn't give an inch to whatever these bastards threw at me. The vest I was wearing wasn't just for show. It had plates front and back, as well as some covering the sides. They were made with boron carbide, one of the hardest materials on earth.

There was a .45 in a shoulder rig, and one on my hip. A compact Glock 9mm was strapped to my ankle. Strapped across my chest was a pump-action shotgun with dual tube magazines currently holding eleven shells of 00 buckshot. Across my back, I had a compact submachine gun loaded with 4.6x30mm armor-piercing cartridges, forty of them, all nestled into a box magazine. Also belted to my hip was a knife with a fixed blade that was six inches long and razor-sharp.

The club was tucked away in a part of Dearborn not recognized by the tourism bureau. A strip of cheap motels, hookers, tattoo parlors and head shops.

I'd parked the Maverick right in front of the place and now I walked right under the neon sign and straight through the entrance.

Immediately, pounding rock music greeted me, along with the smell of booze, cigarettes and cheap perfume.

Two meatheads in black suits reached for their guns and I shot them both and walked right on by. Over the music, I thought I heard someone scream but it was hard to tell.

A drunk girl on stage was barely dancing

and beyond I spotted a long hallway at the back of the main room. I walked past a couple of drunk guys who still had on their air-conditioning repairman shirts and reached the hallway. Two doors off to my left were the restrooms. Straight ahead, a door had just opened and inside, I'd seen some lockers and a couple of the dancers in the act of changing costumes, or maybe shooting up. It was hard to tell.

That left the door on my right marked "PRIVATE." I walked up to it, rapped on it with the butt of my gun and waited. Eventually, it opened a crack and I shot right through it, pulled the door open and walked inside. The guard was on the ground and I shot him in the head. The door slammed shut behind me.

Straight ahead of me was a tacky lounge area, with velvet couches and leather chairs. There were side tables holding ashtrays and half-filled cocktail glasses. Smoke hung in the air.

Someone had just left, and quickly.

I moved quickly through the lounge, and into the bar area. A girl was hiding underneath the bar. "Get out," I said.

She squirmed out and ran past me.

To the right was a hallway with two rooms branching off from it. The first door was half ajar. Standing to the left of the door, using the wall as a shield, I reached forward and gave the door a quick push.

It exploded simultaneously with the sound of multiple gunshots. Heavy rounds. A revolver. After the sixth shot I pivoted into the doorway with my shotgun and fired three rounds in a burst straight into the chest of a man who was literally blown off his feet and straight back into the wall. He slid down, leaving a giant smear of blood on the beige paint.

Just to be sure, I walked in and looked at his face. He was the one on the other playing card.

Which left Jibril. Or Gabriel. The most powerful angel ever.

Yeah, well, I thought. *I'm the angel of death and Gabriel's time is running out.*

At the next door, I switched from the shotgun to the submachine gun.

"Come in, August High," a voice called. "I am unarmed."

The door slowly swung open and there he

was. Jibril. Head of the ALM. He was almost as big as me with a thick beard and hairy arms. The room was empty, save for a table and a packing crate. There were blocks stacked neatly in some kind of latex sheath. Waterproof no doubt.

I entered the room and moved to the right. His eyes tracked me.

"You do not disappoint," he said. "A drink?"

In the silence that followed, he shrugged. "You can join us. Or fight me with your bare hands. Or, the obvious choice, shoot me like a coward."

He did a three-hundred-and-sixty-degree turn, to show he didn't have a weapon.

Calmly, I reached back, closed the door and locked it.

"Yes, you are honorable!" he cried out.

I put down both of the long guns and set them on the floor, along with both of my .45s and I shrugged off the vest, also dropping it to the floor. Finally, I tossed my knife onto the pile, along with my ankle gun.

Jibril took a step toward me, his movements fluid and controlled, like a predator sizing up its prey.

In retrospect, his strategy had a flaw. It was clear he expected some kind of final epic fight that in movies, would go on for a good ten minutes. Hundreds of punches that never seemed to do any damage, bodies being thrown through windows, kicks to the head that never knocked anyone out, lots of corny dialogue and finally, a sweaty, exhausted winner.

To be honest, I never was a big fan of those types of movies.

In my head, a totally different scenario unfolded. Pops would have been pissed off at me but I didn't care.

All I could think about was Holla strung up like a deer, Lee Robson staked to the wall, and Monroe. Beautiful, sexy, smart Monroe.

So I walked straight into his punches.

Oh, he hit me. And they were solid, powerful shots. One cracked me right on the cheekbone, another just below my ear, and yet another, right in the solar plexus.

They didn't slow me down one bit.

Now I was inside him and he rocked my body with short hooks. Left. Right. Left. Right. But by then, I was on him. Pops had been right. I'd been the biggest baby in that orphanage. Everything about me was huge.

Including my head.

The average human head weighs around eleven pounds.

Mine might not be double that, but it probably wasn't far off. If anyone deserved being called a bonehead, it was me.

So when I snapped my neck forward and crashed my oversized cranium right into his nose, it did some serious damage.

He was tough, though, I'll give him that. He tried to hook a leg behind mine and push me over but that was never going to happen. Good idea. Impossible to execute.

My left hand shot to his throat, my fingers able to touch at the back. Jibril's eyes widened, thinking I was going to choke him.

Wrong again.

I turned slightly and crashed a short right into his already broken nose. Something strange happened then. It looked as if most of his nose, which was sizeable, had been actually driven *inside* his face. It looked almost concave. A spurt of blood and goop erupted from his left eye.

The same right hand hit him in the same spot.

And then again.

And again.

And again.

After the fifth punch, my giant fist came away dripping blood and a bunch of other stuff.

Jibril's face was pretty much gone. A mangled, bloody, pulped ball of meat sat atop his neck, which I had crushed in my grip.

At that point, of all the dead people I'd seen, he looked the deadest.

I turned, still holding his neck and threw him across the load of drugs. I retrieved my knife to cut a length of rope tied around the crate. I looped one end over an exposed beam in the ceiling and the other around Jibril's ankle, which I then carefully knotted. It wasn't difficult at all to hoist the dead man up. I tied off the other end to the shipping crate itself, which probably weighed twice as much as Jibril.

The big man now hung in the center of the room. I reached out, held his body still, and sliced off his shirt, revealing his bare torso. Next, I plunged my knife into his lower stomach, just above the belt, and pulled downward until I felt it hit his sternum. I pulled the knife out, and most of Jibril's guts came with it.

Taking a step back to avoid the blood, I heard something behind me.

I turned and standing in the doorway, the key hanging in the door, was the young man from the convenience store.

Malik.

In his hand was a revolver, pointing at the ground.

He began to raise it and I could see his hand shake as he did so.

I stepped toward him, raised the knife and threw it. The big blade buried itself in Malik's throat. His hand must have reflexively clenched because he squeezed off a shot that went into the floor five feet from me.

He stumbled, and then fell.

Quickly, I shrugged on the vest, got all of my weapons back into place, went to Malik and dug my knife out of his throat, making sure to cut it all the way open.

"Should have stuck to working in retail," I said to his corpse.

CHAPTER
TWENTY

TWO MONTHS LATER

Summer was over and the first cool nights came to Michigan. It was the time of year plenty of people loved. Football season, leaves on the trees changing color, fires in the fireplace.

Standing over Monroe's grave, it didn't feel good at all.

Selena Monroe, it said just above the dates of her birth and death.

Simple, but elegant. Just like the woman herself.

This wasn't my first time coming to see

her, so I had already told her about what I'd done to the people who'd put her here. I provided plenty of detail, maybe too much, but I wanted her to know their departure from this world had been very, very messy.

I set a bouquet of flowers next to her headstone and told her goodbye.

As I walked back to the Maverick, I thought about what I'd read in the paper this morning. A stunning news story revealing a massacre in Iraq years ago, perpetrated by a rogue group of ex-Iraqi Army special ops soldiers. The article went on to provide details on how the fallout from that fateful event had bled over into Detroit, quite literally.

The story was a sensation, and it was only the first installment.

The writer, a now famous reporter named Gretchen Mercer, promised there was much, much more of the story to tell.

My name would not be mentioned as I had requested.

Something told me she would keep her word.

It was a story that would probably captivate readers for many months, and then would quietly fade into the background.

Not a bad thing.

Sometimes, that's all I wanted to do.

Fade into the background.

THE END

BUY THE NEXT BOOK IN THE SERIES

HIGH VELOCITY: August High Thriller
Book 2

CLICK HERE TO BUY

A USA TODAY BESTSELLING BOOK

Book One in The JACK REACHER Cases

CLICK HERE TO BUY NOW

FRANCES NEAGLEY & JACK REACHER'S SPECIAL INVESTIGATORS

CLICK HERE TO BUY BOOK ONE
IN THIS THRILLING NEW SERIES

AN AWARD-WINNING BESTSELLING MYSTERY SERIES

Buy DEAD WOOD, the first John Rockne Mystery.

CLICK HERE TO BUY

"Fast-paced, engaging, original."
-*NYTimes bestselling author Thomas Perry*

ABOUT THE AUTHOR

Dan Ames is a USA TODAY Bestselling Author, Amazon Kindle #1 bestseller, GoodReads Readers Choice finalist and winner of the Independent Book Award for Crime Fiction.

www.authordanames.com
dan@authordanames.com

ALSO BY DAN AMES

THE JACK REACHER CASES

The JACK REACHER Cases #1 (A Hard Man To Forget)

The JACK REACHER Cases #2 (The Right Man For Revenge)

The JACK REACHER Cases #3 (A Man Made For Killing)

The JACK REACHER Cases #4 (The Last Man To Murder)

The JACK REACHER Cases #5 (The Man With No Mercy)

The JACK REACHER Cases #6 (A Man Out For Blood)

The JACK REACHER Cases #7 (A Man Beyond The Law)

The JACK REACHER Cases #8 (The Man Who Walks Away)

The JACK REACHER Cases (The Man Who Strikes Fear)

The JACK REACHER Cases (The Man Who Stands Tall)

The JACK REACHER Cases (The Man Who Works Alone)

The Jack Reacher Cases (A Man Built For Justice)

The JACK REACHER Cases #13 (A Man Born for Battle)

The JACK REACHER Cases #14 (The Perfect Man for Payback)

The JACK REACHER Cases #15 (The Man Whose Aim Is True)

The JACK REACHER Cases #16 (The Man Who Dies Here)

The JACK REACHER Cases #17 (The Man With Nothing To Lose)

The JACK REACHER Cases #18 (The Man Who Never Goes Back)

The JACK REACHER Cases #19 (The Man From The Shadows)

The JACK REACHER CASES #20 (The Man Behind The Gun)

The JACK REACHER Cases #21 (The Man Who Went To War)

JACK REACHER'S SPECIAL INVESTIGATORS

BOOK ONE: DEAD MEN WALKING

BOOK TWO: GAME OVER

BOOK THREE: LIGHTS OUT

BOOK FOUR: NEVER FORGIVE, NEVER FORGET

BOOK FIVE: HIT THEM FAST, HIT THEM HARD

BOOK SIX: FINISH THE FIGHT

BOOK SEVEN: THE WAY OUT

BOOK EIGHT: EASY TO KILL

THE JOHN ROCKNE MYSTERIES

DEAD WOOD (John Rockne Mystery #1)

HARD ROCK (John Rockne Mystery #2)

COLD JADE (John Rockne Mystery #3)

LONG SHOT (John Rockne Mystery #4)

EASY PREY (John Rockne Mystery #5)

BODY BLOW (John Rockne Mystery #6)

THE WADE CARVER THRILLERS

MOLLY (Wade Carver Thriller #1)

SUGAR (Wade Carver Thriller #2)

ANGEL (Wade Carver Thriller #3)

THE WALLACE MACK THRILLERS

THE KILLING LEAGUE (Wallace Mack Thriller #1)

THE MURDER STORE (Wallace Mack Thriller #2)

FINDERS KILLERS (Wallace Mack Thriller #3)

THE MARY COOPER MYSTERIES

DEATH BY SARCASM (Mary Cooper Mystery #1)

MURDER WITH SARCASTIC INTENT (Mary Cooper Mystery #2)

GROSS SARCASTIC HOMICIDE (Mary Cooper Mystery #3)

THE CIRCUIT RIDER (WESTERNS)

THE CIRCUIT RIDER (Circuit Rider #1)
KILLER'S DRAW (Circuit Rider #2)

THE RAY MITCHELL THRILLERS

THE RECRUITER

KILLING THE RAT

HEAD SHOT

STANDALONE THRILLERS:

KILLER GROOVE (Rockne & Cooper Mystery #1)

BEER MONEY (Burr Ashland Mystery #1)

TO FIND A MOUNTAIN (A WWII Thriller)

BOX SETS:

AMES TO KILL

GROSSE POINTE PULP

GROSSE POINTE PULP 2

TOTAL SARCASM

WALLACE MACK THRILLER COLLECTION

SHORT STORIES:

THE GARBAGE COLLECTOR

BULLET RIVER

SCHOOL GIRL

HANGING CURVE

SCALE OF JUSTICE

FREE BOOKS AND MORE

Would you like a FREE copy
of my story BULLET RIVER and the chance
to win a free Kindle?

Then sign up for the DAN AMES BOOK CLUB:

For special offers and new releases, sign up here

Printed in Great Britain
by Amazon